AFRICAN SAMSON

By HUMPHREY HARMAN

In the valley of Kano, the land of No, near Lake Victoria, the plain is littered with great gray stones, rolled down long ago from the steep slopes above, the pieces left over when Asis made the hills. But there too, resting alone beneath a wild fig tree, is a big black boulder of a quite different kind, smooth and polished and hard and looking something like a sleeping seal. To a man with time, a whole kind of person with time to live and talk, Opio, who dwelt near the rock, might tell the story of Magere the Stone. After all he had been part of it.

The story began when Opio was a boy, many years after No, Opio's grandfather, had led the Joluo people to the valley. There they lived in peace, until the Nandi, herdsmen-warriors of the hills, began raiding the Joluo cattle. They came at night, when all Joluo stayed within the great ojuok hedges of their bomas, and they took only a few cattle at a time, just to keep the fun going. But one day, when Opio discovered a band of Nandi hiding among the rocks with their loot, his uncle Magere shamed enough Joluo into fighting to gain a great victory. And from that morning, Magere became a legend.

Again and again, he led the Joluo against their enemies, gaining riches and great fame. He was heedless of knife and spear thrusts; nothing could wound him, and he became known as Magere the Stone. It was not until he married the beautiful Nandi girl Tapkesos, when it seemed that peace had come at last between the two tribes, that the secret of his strength became his undoing.

The similarity of this tale to that of the Biblical Samson is an intriguing enigma, but to the Joluo people it is all fact. Whether fact or legend, Mr. Harman's splendid story is so convincingly human and so true in its detail—the day-to-day life in the bomas, the hot emptiness of the stony landscape, the awesome vastness of Nyanza, the Lake—that it becomes a memorable reading experience.

AFRICAN SAMSON

Humphrey Harman

AFRICAN SAMSON

THE VIKING PRESS NEW YORK

Published in 1966 by The Viking Press, Inc.
625 Madison Avenue, New York, N. Y. 10022

Published in England
under title *Black Samson*

Library of Congress catalog card number: AC 66–10782

Fic 1. Africa
2. Legends—Africa, East

PRINTED IN THE U. S. A.

Contents

AFRICAN SAMSON

The Black Rock

1

They call it Victoria on the maps, but to the people who live there it is Nyanza, or, as we would say, the Lake.

The point of the name lives in its simplicity, for the people of Africa have a talent, little realized by the world as yet, for finding the sixpence in the corner when it comes to words. Here, they imply that there are other lakes. Elmenteita, for instance, like an emerald on its tortured volcanic floor, or Hannington, a gloomy sulphur-smelling slit among barren hills. Many others, all describable. But this one! An ocean inside a continent. A world, for it includes all the provinces watered by the rain the sun sucks from it, all people who turn to it, all history, all legend. There is no rival, no adequate description possible or required. It is the Lake.

No man, of course, knows the whole of it. Not even the steamer captains who take their slow, panting boats from one sun-deluged port to another, not even the naked fishermen who go down to it each day in bleached canoes with patched and ragamuffin sails, nor the hundreds of tribes who live along its shores and on its islands.

It is too big. One must be content with a part. Kano will do.

Kano is a wide valley running into an eastern gulf in the lake's shore, there called Kavirondo. It is flat and hot and usually dry. Pretty barren now, for the goats have eaten it naked and the soil has gone into the lake, but those who know say that it was once beautiful with grass growing higher than a man's shoulder.

Opio was one of those who knew.

Opio lived in Kano some ten years ago. His tribe was called the Joluo and he did not know his age, for he held to an old belief of his people which is that to number anything of value, children or cattle, or the years of a life, is an unlucky thing to do. But he could have been ninety then, perhaps a little more, which was indeed a great age for a man of his time and place. He was shrunken and frail, with a face as lined as the glaze of an old plate. A very gentle, friendly man, who loved to talk. He lived a dozen miles from the shore of the lake and one or other of his granddaughters came each day to cook his dinner and see if he needed anything else.

But Opio needed very little. He had almost entirely stopped living forward. He preferred the past. In Africa history has a habit of coming up as far as the time your father was a boy. With Opio it was right at his elbow. He talked familiarly of men who came out of legend, as if they might be expected to appear that moment from the deep shadow of a hut doorway. It was unnerving to sit and listen to him and at the same time see the telegraph poles following the great road across the plain, and hear the heavy, flat-footed tread of machinery in the sugar mills at nearby Miwani.

His hut was the usual round-walled, deep-thatched house of those parts. Neater than most. I never went into it because one does not sit in a house to talk. Out-of-doors is the place where living is done. Close to it was a black rock.

The plain was littered with great stones there, rolled down long ago from the steep slopes above, the pieces left over when Asis made the hills. But these were gray and of the same crumbling rock as the precipices above, one that grows rotten under the fierce rain and sun of Kano. This black boulder was of quite a different kind, smooth and polished and hard, and it squatted alone beneath a fine wild fig tree and looked somewhat like a sleeping seal. The Joluo people knew all about that stone, its story and reason for being there. When they passed they sometimes slapped its smooth sides affectionately, and often brought a collection of tools and weapons to sharpen against it. The hardness gave a quicker edge to a knife or spear than other stones.

Sometimes strangers who had heard of the story were curious enough to leave their cars on the great trunk road and, asking their way at the huts they passed, come by winding paths to the stone. There they would stare for a few moments, disappointed perhaps that there was not more to be seen. For it was only a black boulder crouching in the goat-cropped grass and all about was the familiar Africa they had walked through.

Opio kept a close watch on it. This was quite understandable because, as you will see, it contained much of his life. Besides, he had little else to do but sit in the sun and wait for what the rock brought him. When he saw a guest (for he regarded visitors in this light) he would hurry forward, looking ragged and uncertain, like a bird that is learning to fly. He would make a formal greeting, sit at a little distance and ask slow questions.

Time is plentiful and free as air in Africa. It is boorish not to use it. Opio had all the courtesy of his people and his gentle conversation went round and round while he found out if you were a whole kind of person, with time to live and talk to guardians of rocks, or merely a creature in a hurry.

If you were the former you might get the story of the stone.

But there had to be time, for, like the conversation that preceded it, the story also meandered. Much like the river that runs through Kano, great curves like a snake in the dust and sometimes broken into a necklace of pools with no river between.

And it began in the beginning, back enough in years for Opio to take sights on his story and hit it firmly.

It began with his "grandfather," a famous man in his way, who was called No.

Magere

1

He never saw his grandfather because No died before Opio was born. But, of course, he knew all about him. Everyone did, for he was No, the man who led the first of their people to make homes on Kano and there were many songs invented about him. Not perhaps as many as there were about Ramogi, who brought the Joluo people from Uganda, or Toll, who was a magician as well as a warrior, or Sakwa, who founded a tribe. But enough to make certain that his life would not be forgotten; especially by a grandson.

When No was young, a boy in a great family, all turbulent and touchy, held together only by a strong and sometimes terrible old man, the people were in slow movement round the northern shores of the Great Lake. His clan was one of many, and they lived in Sakwa, with the old forests on one side of them, and the marshes and the lake on the other. The family lived in a dozen houses with smooth walls and yellow thatch, enclosed by a great hedge of ojuok. The gateway was made of whole tree trunks, bleached by sun and rain, and by it a pile of beams and thorn boughs, higher than a house, which were dragged across each night to close the way. Inside the head of the clan sat on a fine polished stool, his cowskin cloak reaching to the ground, and daughters and servants were as busy as hens when the morning handful of grain is scattered. Outside the hedge, the huts of his tenants stretched as far as could be seen, and children herded goats on small rock-covered hills, and young men speared pig among the reeds.

A great and strong household, and it was well that it was, for the times were troubled, full of war and men going and coming, looking for land and glory and easy wealth.

Sometimes a band of them came along the lake shore, strangers with hungry eyes upon the tall corn in the fields, but also taking note of the strong young men and the spears they carried. Then they would speak politely, mention a relative by marriage from a distant clan, and eat the porridge they were given, with their hosts looking on silently, and make their thanks and go, carrying their hyena grins to where the taking would be easier.

But in those days, when there was always empty land or weak clans beyond, such a household lasted only so long as there was one man strong enough to hold it. When the father died the sons fell out, and scattered, looking for something better than a share. After the women had wailed at this clan leader's death, No and his brothers, a round dozen of them, bickered over the land.

"Take it!" cried No at last in a passion. "I'll not live my life cackling over one corner of a field, or a share of six blades of grass between rocks. I'll go and get something of my own. Who'll follow?"

He had strength and cunning and a cold eye of command, had No, and because of these many did follow. A younger brother, some tenants' sons who hoped for fat farms and saw no hope of getting them in Sakwa; perhaps fifty men in all.

These warriors went first, leaving the women and children to follow when they were sent for. They went south along the lake shore and found it settled by their own people. No looked with envy at the fields and well-made houses and remembered the young men who had come visiting from the west in his youth. These same houses and fields might well have belonged to some of those men. Then he laughed and said, "As I'm thinking now, so they thought then."

Presently they came to where the lake took a great bite inland and here the high blue hills to the north came near to the water's edge. But the land was starveling, great slabs of red rock falling in broken steps to the beach, with aloes growing in the crevices. A land made for lizards and snakes, not men, and indeed snakes were plentiful and No lost a man from a cobra's bite.

It was here that some of his followers grew fainthearted and began to grumble, but No laughed at them and beat the worst of the mutterers with the butt of his spear, and so they all went on round the corner of the hills and came to where a great valley ran east.

It was immense, broad and deep and flat, the hills about high and sheltering, and at this time, just after the long rains, the grass stood waist-high between the figs and thorns and cork trees. Down the valley, strong-flowing and winding, a river ran to the lake, and on the quiet surface of one of its great curves they noticed, at evening, many spreading rings. Fish were feeding, and the sight gave them deep satisfaction, for the Joluo are a waterside people who hunger for fish.

Best of all, the land was empty. They moved cautiously about it for a week and found no one. Not even a hunter's dead fire.

They built shelters of grass and thorn beside the river and sent half their number back to Sakwa with news of their find, and to help with the harvest and later the new planting, for the women were alone and would be hard pressed to get the work done. The rest, No and his brother, a man called Okoth, and twenty-five of their followers, stayed to try out the new country, for they had the caution of their people. It was true that it was empty now, but who could tell if people had not lived there in the past, and whether the ghosts of their ancestors would not be active and resent newcomers? They waited to see, and lived on fish and an occasional hog or buck, speared when it came to drink at evening. They waited a year and grew thin and longed for good maize porridge, but nothing worse troubled them.

Then, when the rains came again, they dug a small field and sowed millet and beans and watched to see what harvest they got. It was a good harvest and, indeed, no misfortune of any kind occurred during this time.

Then No decided to move. He left Okoth and some few

others and went back with the rest to Sakwa. There he consulted the ancestors through the witch doctors and all the signs were good. He paid a good bull for this information, but it was worth the price. Then he left his clan and, followed by his family and servants and cattle, he went to the valley that his people had already named Kano, the land of No. A great many of his father's tenants came also, especially the landless sort, for they reckoned that No was a good man to follow, and it was generally admitted that he had managed the whole business with wisdom and prudence. No promised them holdings in Kano if they would be his men, and altogether about three hundred men, women and children moved there with a great number of cattle. They arrived just before the rains, a year after the place had been discovered, and squatted along the river and it was a busy time building houses and settling fights over new fields.

When they were at home and beginning to be comfortable Okoth talked one evening with his brother. They were outside No's new house, the freshly planted slips of ojuok which would make the great hedge just beginning to sprout, and the sun near setting. The light was strange and because of this the hills seemed to have moved closer and the shaggy fur of trees covering their tops was plain to see. Okoth looked at them and said, "I wonder what's *there*."

"Oh, bah!" replied his brother. "What have hills to do with a Luo?"

The question had point, for the Joluo are a plains people, and hate the hills.

2

If Okoth had lived a little longer than he did he would not have asked his question about the hills. He would have known what was in them.

The brothers had lived good lives and given land to their people and each founded clans, for although the new country took No's name, the followers of each brother lived separately. There was no quarreling between them, for both had plenty of room, but No's people clung as close to the lake's edge as they could, while Okoth's built their farms along the river further up the valley. When the brothers died, and this happened within a few years of each other, they were buried in their clan lands and the people held these the firmer for it. Now, they said, both No and Okoth would always be there to keep a watchful eye upon their interests.

There was peace for more than twenty years afterward. It is true that in one year there was a little trouble with the Kisii, a people who lived on the southern flank of the valley, but it was settled without much fighting, and since there were many miles of empty land and rugged hills between the tribes, there seemed no reason why they should not live quietly together.

After No there were no more great leaders, for none were needed. The great tangled hedges round the houses were kept repaired for nothing more serious than a hyena prowling after goats, and folk tilled their land and grazed their cattle contentedly and only asked of their neighbors that they dance and feast with them at weddings or join to mourn with them when a man died. At other times they were most approved of if they minded their own business. Although the Joluo have a deep sense of being one special people they live most contentedly with a little elbow room and quarrel less if they meet their neighbors when they choose to do so.

So, many peaceful happy years went by with the red cowhide shields growing dusty on the rafters of the huts and the flocks and herds growing larger. There were many children about the homesteads and, better still, they thrived. Only the old men, some of them, who had finished with work and now sucked their long pipes in the shadow of the eaves, sometimes complained that the world grew soft, and that it was scarcely possible to distinguish men from women.

Opio was one of those children who thrived. He was born in a farm deep in the valley and his father was Onyango, the eldest son of Okoth, and his mother Anyango, from Gem, for when the clansmen did not marry the daughters of their tenants they went far, even to distant Alego and Gem, for their wives. It was a good farm, with deep black soil that held the rain and grew maize twice as tall as a man. The household hedge was close-set and within it were five great huts: a large one, where his father and mother lived, and others which belonged to his grandmother, his uncle Magere and Opio's two elder sisters. An old herdsman called Odongo and his wife lived with them, and there were other, smaller, shelters where Odongo's two sons, calves, chickens and occasional benighted visitors slept in a haphazard kind of way. Houses were only for sleeping in, after all; by day, old or young worked, ate or napped out of doors.

Opio's grandmother was called Adero and she was a strong-minded old woman with a tongue to match her opinions. She was really the head of the household, though Opio's father thought he was, and, of course, he was in name. In Opio's earliest memory it was Adero who set the world turning each morning, the girls to grinding corn in stone mortars, to coaxing fires, fetching water and boiling porridge. The boys were packed off with the goats and sheep to pasture and, later, Odongo to the river to water the cattle.

When Opio was small he was carried on his mother's back or lay on a small square of cowhide in the shadow of a bush while she worked in the gardens, but when he grew old enough to walk, bandy as an ant bear, he played all day near Adero's house, and she would give him a handful of bright red beans to catch his eye, and slap him when he put them in his mouth. When he walked sturdily without falling he went free for a few years, with Odongo's boys and the goats and sheep, to the river with the women, swimming doglike in the shallow creeks and pools, to the cattle boma where the soft-churned mud was a favorite toy. His meals were got by asking for them from whomever he found eating, and at night he slept with the boys, or in his uncle's house, or with his grandmother, whichever happened to be the nearest when sleep overcame him. When he spent the night with Adero she told him stories before he slept, which he loved but which often filled his sleep with dreams. Stories always meant much to him. They stayed with him longer than was usual with most children, the terror and laughter of them lasting into the bright day when others forgot. And when he was a man folk would walk ten miles for the pleasure of hearing Opio's stories.

In the year that Opio was born the steep hills round Kano answered Okoth's question as to what was in them.

They were not empty. They were the home of the Nandi, a people hardly farmers at all, but herdsmen and warriors. They were tall and lean and fierce and they believed that in the beginning Asis had given them all the cattle in the world. It was for them a most convenient belief because from it they argued that everyone else who had cattle was only minding them until the Nandi wanted them back. And what the Nandi enjoyed most in all the world was taking them back.

From the hills, the forests on their tops and the rocks tumbled on their slopes, the Nandi watched the new farms being built below. For years it was only scouts and hunting parties who watched, for they also were a people in movement and had not yet filled the land they were to call Nandi. Generation after generation they had moved through the forest, grazing cattle in the long glades, making small clearings for the sowing of millet. This they needed for beer-making and it was the only crop they grew. When the land grew poor they moved on, leaving it to recover. Presently the forests ended and the plain spread open below.

The Joluo in the valley had cows. It was true that they were not very good ones because the land was low and hot, but that year the Nandi began to take them, a few at a time, so as to keep the fun going.

And they came at night.

To the Joluo this was the most frightening thing about the Nandi. That they came at night, when the owl flies bringing bad luck and the hyena chuckles over its secrets and the world draws in. A time which cries for the comfort of fires and solid walls. But it was then the Nandi came, and women would snatch up their children and run with them tucked under their arms to the sheltering rocks. The tall young men whose ostrich plumes made them giants would break the cattle fence and whistle softly to calm the frightened beasts before driving them away. And maybe, before they did so, fire the thatch of a house or so, just for a light to work by.

It was never a big raid. Just one homestead here and, a month or so later, another there. A little like striking lightning, something that happened to a distant neighbor but never, it was to be hoped, oneself. In the morning a man would not mind walking a mile or so to see the mess and talk about it, and even stay to give a hand rebuilding.

But as for doing anything about it, what was there to to do? Fight? Who can fight the hills and forests? Go? But the land was good and where they came from there was no more to be had and who wanted to return and be the servants of relations?

Besides, this was their Kano.

The matter stayed where it was in the list of griefs that were naturally part of a man's life: storm, flood and sickness, the locusts which blackened the sky, and the little looped worm which in some years crawled in millions and ate the corn to the ground. The people of No and Okoth stayed where they were and made the best of life, which, if it was sometimes hard, could also often be good.

3

When Opio was still a little boy he was given another name. He was called Opio the Fish and the name came to him in this way.

The Kano River was usually a quiet and friendly one. But several times a year, when the rain fell heavily in the distant hills, it changed its nature and bellowed like a bull and came out of its bed and in at the door of your house if you had not been wise about where you built. This was a time of some grumbling and a good deal more laughing, for to be wet on Kano was a matter the sun soon cured. Also at flood times the river was full of a tiny silver fish which could always be caught by anchoring basket traps in the right places. Then afterward the fish were boiled and pounded and eaten, heads, tails and all. A fine rich food with a strong smell and salty tang which was loved the better because it appeared in the pot for only a few weeks a year.

This year the rains had been unusually heavy and the fish came in such quantities as had never been seen before. The strong-flowing muddy water glittered with their millions and everyone went to the river with pots and baskets to gather them, and sticks to beat the water and drive them to the traps. Men, women and children joined hands and waded up to their waists fighting the current, splashing and beating and screaming with laughter when anyone was swept from his feet and went downstream with his heels in the air.

Opio went too and played the part his size and strength permitted, taking his place in the lines near the bank where the water was shallow and did not wrestle so hard with a man. But after an hour or so of this he grew tired and left the fun and wandered up the bank away from the clamor.

Presently he reached a tiny muddy creek and sat at the water's edge beneath the shade of a tree.

And there he saw the fish. He saw it gradually because, although it was only a few inches below the surface, it was lying on mud and was the color of mud and almost invisible. But presently the eyes moved and Opio saw it all.

For a moment he stared unbelieving. It was big, longer than his arm. Then he got carefully to his feet and bent slowly with hand outstretched to grab, at which moment the undercut earth bank he stood on crumbled beneath his weight and he fell clawing onto the fish.

It was not a mere arm's length. Most was buried in the mud and it was as long and heavy as a man, a great mud-fish, strong and dangerous, with a bite that would go through a man's foot and leave him a cripple for life.

Opio was lucky. Ordinarily it would have either savaged him and gone, or shaken him off like a dog shaking dew from its coat. But it was deep-bedded in silt and most of the first flurry was spent in freeing itself, and by the time that had happened Opio had a grasp of the fleshy bags beneath the eyes and his feet locked round. He hung on. The hard greasy body beneath him exploded with power and he shut his eyes and felt sick with panic—and hung on.

The fish floundered in the shallow water of the creek for a moment, then lunged out for the river proper. There also it was shallow, the water tumbling over stone steps covered in mud, and the fish scraped the bottom and twice rammed the bank. Opio dug his fingers in folds of leathery flesh and hung on tighter. He opened his mouth to cry for help and was half drowned with black silt-heavy water.

And so, a moment later, the people fishing below saw a monstrous creature coming down the shallows above them, half fish, half boy, now arched out of the water in a welter of foam, now vanished beneath with a swirl. A great shout of laughter went up, for, on that day, when everything caused laughter, nothing had been seen funnier than this.

But one or two saw the danger to the boy and the profit to be made, and Magere, Opio's uncle, was one. He snatched a spear from the bank and after leaping up the shallows waited for boy and fish to come to him. When they were at his knees he shouted, "Leave it, Opio!" and Opio, seeing the man standing above and the raised spear wheeling black against the sky, hearing nothing but the roaring of water, but feeling that all was now in other hands, let go. His hands and knees went slack and the current plucked him away and waiting hands gathered him lower down and put him on the bank to dry.

Magere stabbed the fish and came down also in a flurry, holding the snapping beast at spear's length, until others finished the business for him.

So that day the family and their neighbors feasted on mudfish, for the flesh is good, dark and grained like meat, not white and flaked as might be expected. And Opio became his uncle's favorite nephew.

But, of course, he was no longer just Opio. He was Opio the Fish.

4

That same year, after the millet harvest, a number of young Nandi planned a cattle raid on Kano. They came from the Soina Hills, just above Kano on the northern side, and their leader was named Chelegat, who was regarded by many as a warrior with a future.

When the plan was hatched at night, round a fire outside a cattle boma, Chelegat produced a new and daring idea.

"Let us," he said, "go right down as far as the people who live beside the lake."

His hearers jeered.

"Walk thirty miles for a cow! When a hundred are to be had down *there* for the taking!"

"Why indeed?" said the rest. "Since when have you loved walking, Chelegat?"

"No, listen!" cried Chelegat. "Listen, Kipsaina. I'm talking sense. The valley cattle are worked out. Look at last year. We came back with six beasts whose ribs were only good for playing tunes on. The Moi clan raided up the valley a month ago. Did you see the catch they brought back? I asked them what they wanted with a pack of Luo dogs. It's true. The girls still bark when they see them. I tell you that if they were ever worth the walk they're worked out now. But down by the lake they'll be fatter. The grass is good down there, and also"—he grinned—"the lakeside farmers will be fatter too, and not expecting guests.

Oh, the lakeside cows
Are fat as sows,
And the lakeside Luo fatter. . . ."

Here he kicked up his heels and rolled on the turf at the aptness of his own versifying.

"Ape," said Kipsaina. "But maybe there's something in what you say."

"Of course there is!" cried Chelegat, growing serious. "Now listen. We'll take Kibii and Kiprono and . . ." and they all hitched forward on their hunkers, put their heads together and began to plan.

Thirty men went and Chelegat was named the leader. It was a trifling affair; the men came from no more than a dozen families and so there was no need to ask the approval of the elders who ruled the clan. Indeed they thought so little of it that not even a sheep was sacrificed to bring luck and this was to be remembered later. They waited a week until the moon was gone and then they painted for war and set out. They took shields and spears and simis—the long leaflike iron swords bought from the Nyangori smiths—but they left behind the leathern war-bags which were usually carried on raids, filled with raw damp millet flour pressed down hard. They only intended to spend two days over the business and a Nandi can go that time hungry and fight the better for it.

Down the slopes leading to the plain they loped, one

behind the other in the evening light, following the winding buck paths that led to the river. From a kite's view above they would have seemed more like a black snake than thirty men. Each peered from his halo of black-and-white colobus fur at the naked back of the man in front, and trusted to Chelegat. What else was a leader for?

On the plain the darkness became absolute and they sent out scouts and moved cautiously, keeping touch with each other by the gentle whisper the long fur anklet each man wore on his right leg made against the dry grass. The scouts moved by the stars and the rest by the faint sounds of their passage. They made for the river first and then followed it in the direction of the lake. Not near, because of the farms thick along its banks, but parallel to the course. When they could not hear the water they could smell it, and occasionally, by crouching low, they could see the faint loom of riverside trees, a deeper blackness in the black sky. Sometimes they padded over the broken ground and short stubble of fields and once a dog came snarling through the night from a hut and its clamor ended with a spear-thrust. They carried the body a mile before burying it in an ant bear's hole. It would save anyone asking questions in the morning.

All night they trotted, never speaking, and near morning they quickened the pace, worried that dawn would catch them in the open plain. But all went well and by the time a face could be seen they were hidden in a deep sea of reeds at the lake's edge.

They stayed there all day, sleeping or drowsing on their impudent backs, chewing young reed stems, or playing complicated games with the black-and-red beans of the cork tree, which they tossed up by the handful and caught on their knuckles. They called the score in whispers and rolled on their backs, shaking with silent laughter when they won. Occasionally a man crawled on his stomach to where the reeds stood in water and filled a gourd and returned to share it with the rest. A sentry lay flat at the edge of the marsh and watched the villages. He saw the cooking fires lit and yawning children stumble out driving goats before them and women carrying heavy digging sticks to the fields. Later he saw the men drive the cattle inland to grass and the sentry judged their worth with a keen eye. When they were out of sight he became bored and watched the ants foraging among the roots between his elbows, and yawned, and waited for the man who would relieve him and let him sleep.

When it was night again the Nandi got to their feet and stretched and set to work.

They burned fourteen houses and the people in them went wailing into the darkness to hide or find shelter in the villages further along the shore. The Nandi, great leaping shadows against the burning huts, ran whooping at their heels. When they had chased them far enough they returned roaring with laughter and gathered a great herd of cattle, the treasured wealth of a dozen families. The youngest calves and a number of worthless old cows they left behind, but the rest they began droving inland through Kano. All that night they herded them gently and skillfully, tapping their flanks lightly with spear butts to keep them bunched, whistling like nightjars to soothe them.

Groups of scouts ran behind and in front and to either side, the ears and eyes of the party; the rest gave no thought to anything but herding, sometimes walking among the beasts with an arm flung across a bull's back.

This was a game they knew and they played it like professionals.

But hurry as they did there is a limit to the speed a cow will move without panic and when dawn came they were still far from the hills and became worried. It was all very well to despise the Joluo by night, but in daylight it might be a different matter. This was the very heart of Luoland; their villages lay scattered round, thick as weeds. By surprise and speed, and the use of their spears, the Nandi believed they could get safely away even in the daylight; but not with the cattle. And they had no taste for the laughter of the girls at home if they returned empty-handed. It seemed best to Chelegat to choose a hiding place, if one could be found upon this loathsome plain, and wait for one more day.

This was done.

They chose a great clutter of rocks, some of them far bigger than houses, all overgrown with scrubby bushes and wild figs whose roots crawled across the stone and vanished into cracks. The place was a home for monkeys and the nimble hyrax and in it they hid the cattle and themselves, and settled down to wait with their spears handy. They were hungry and would dearly have liked to have killed a heifer, but they were fearful that the smoke of a cooking fire might blab of their presence, and they would not eat the meat raw. However, they milked the cows which were in milk, to prevent them from bellowing as well as for food. They drank it fresh, with wry lips, for, to a Nandi, curdled is the only way for milk to be considered drinkable. Curdled with the dryness in it that comes from the charcoal at the bottom of the gourd.

Then they fingered their spears as the sun came up and boasted to each other in whispers. They were a little edgy.

But by midday nothing had happened and then they laughed and felt easier and went to sleep with one of their number watching the cattle, which, having grazed all the morning on the grass between the rocks, were now lying down, chewing their cud in the heat.

Two further sentries drowsed on the top of the greatest rock.

5

Now that morning, as it happened, Opio got up early.

He must have been about ten, although he could not have told you so, since he did not know it. To his people he was not yet a man but decidedly not a child. To be more exact than this was unnecessary and unlucky. His job was to look after his father's flock of sheep and goats and he had been old enough to do that for several years.

He uncurled himself from his bed, which was half an old cowskins laid on the floor beside the hearthstones in Magere's hut, and, without waking anyone, he went outside. It was still dark, but the dawn trembled below the edge of things.

Hardly bothering as yet to open his eyes, he went to his grandmother's house, and there, just inside the door where he knew it would be, was a broken crock filled with cold maize cake. He took two handfuls and leaving the hut with them crossed to the cattle boma. The gate beams were in position, but being small he slipped between them in among the crowded beasts. Near the gate, where he expected him to be, was Chonge, the oldest bull, lying down and breathing heavily into the darkness. Opio sat beside him and huddled his back against warm hide. The bull grunted, but did not look around, and Opio munched his cake, taking bites from first one hand and then the other until it was gone.

When he had finished his meal the sky was lighter and he walked to the boma gate and pulled free the lowest two beams. Then he walked among the sleeping animals, patting the goats and sheep until they got jerkily to their feet. It was not difficult to get them moving. The sheep were stupid, as they always were, for sheep never learn, but the goats knew what was needed and they streamed through the gap in the bottom of the gateway and the sheep followed them. When they were all out Opio replaced the beams. The cows had never stirred. Their time would be later when Odongo would come for them.

Once out of the boma, Mbuzi, the old billy who led the flock, took charge. They did not leave the household by the main entrance, for that was blocked with heavy thorn boughs and would have taken more than Opio's strength to open quickly. Instead they made for a small tunnel-like way through the hedge behind the great house, and through this they jostled, Mbuzi in the lead. Opio caught them up outside and drove them to graze, talking, for the sake of company, to the old billy, who had been his companion on these occasions for as long as he could remember.

Opio wore nothing at all, and he shivered a little in the morning mist, but he was used to that and had only an hour to wait before the sun would put things right. He had a purpose in starting early, for yesterday he had found, in a smooth meadow hidden between rocks, a crop of the great purple-gilled toadstools that his people enjoy best when they are dried and shredded into a stew. He had come on them at evening when there was not time to search properly and now he hoped to find more and have time to do it.

So he stumped on sturdily and when he reached the place where a great maze of gigantic rocks spilled out carelessly on the plain and was overgrown with trees, he left the herd in Mbuzi's charge and set off at once among the rocks. The billy carried a wooden bell round its neck and Opio heard it behind him, its *clock, clock, clock* growing fainter. He knew that the others would not stray beyond the sound, and that there were no gardens nearby to tempt Mbuzi to raid them and bring down angry owners brandishing sticks to warm Opio's rump.

He found the meadow. Nothing remained of the toadstools but scattered broken pieces and a few buttons. The monkeys had been here. He picked a button to nibble, but the rest he left and clambered deeper among the rocks, hoping for a better harvest. A little later he stood on the top of a tall flat rock, having got there by way of a handy tree trunk and a foothold or two for his hard toes.

He straightened himself up, rubbing a knee bruised in the climb . . . and gaped. Below a herd of cattle rested in the shade. Then he saw a tall, near-naked man with a spreading headdress, then another leaning on a spear, and another sleeping . . . and another. . . .

The breath went out of him and he dropped and flattened on the rock.

The herdboys of Africa are fearless. A toddling child will brandish a stick in the face of a lion because right is on his side. The goats are his charge and he believes that nothing, not even a lion, will hurt or rob a child. And, strangely enough, often he is right, and the lion will turn away grumbling, leaving the indignant child in tears, because he has suddenly remembered that he ought to be frightened.

So, when Opio had got over his first shock, and had looked carefully about to discover if he had been seen, he was as full of curiosity as a pumpkin pip, and he stayed and counted the Nandi and the cows. Twenty-eight men he made it, but the cows he gave up. There were far more than he had fingers and toes. Many more. He missed the two sentries who were behind him. Then he went back through the rocks, first on hands and knees, then, when he was out of sight, as fast as his skinny legs would carry him. Forgot the flock and fled like a hare to the world of grown men with his news.

6

Opio's father, Onyango, was away from home, visiting relations in No, and so when he came running, crying that the Nandi were upon them, the man he took the news to was Magere. His uncle was a big, slow-speaking man, and when Opio found him that morning he was putting an edge on a hunting spear with a knob of ironstone. He put down the stone and the spear and listened quietly. The news was only half told when Anyango came home from the river with a pot of water, and seeing Opio where he had no business to be, she seized and shook him, demanding to know what had happened to the flock. Magere told her sharply to stop her noise and let the boy finish his story.

When it was done he went to his house and returned with a great war spear. He told Opio to run with his story to the nearest neighbors, Ochieng and Okello, and tell them to send news to all the clan living beyond the ford on the other side of the river. He was also to say that Magere would see to it that all the people living this side were warned. The men were to gather beneath the great cotton tree, the place where all clan councils were held.

While Opio was listening to what had to be done, hopping from one foot to the other, aching to be gone, Anyango ran from her husband's house, bringing with her the great bull's horn that had belonged to grandfather Okoth and his father before. It was the most precious thing the family possessed and her bringing it was something that could only have happened in the excitement of the moment, for it was not suitable that a woman should so much as touch a war horn. But bring it she did, held before her, rather as if it might bite, and begged Magere to blow and fetch out all the men of the clan.

"And tell every Nandi within earshot that we know they're here?" he said. "Put it back, woman, and find Odongo, and tell him to fetch the cattle back to the boma. He drove them toward the creek this morning."

Then he went off with long strides to play his part and Opio bolted to warn Ochieng and Okello.

And that was how the alarm began.

The excitement gathered slowly because the people lived scattered and because this was Africa, where, in the face of danger, men trust to their instincts rather than their heads. When the ant heap is opened the craving for action spreads slowly, from creature to creature, until in the end even the most distant from the nest stops what it is doing and is ready to bite. So it was here, and some hours later about a hundred and fifty men, some carrying spears, squatted on the bare ground beneath the great tree, and about them a great crowd of women and children.

The trouble was that they were not at all ready to bite. Instead they settled down to something that drew them as the fire draws cats; a good, slow, long, thorough argument.

Opio lay flat along a smooth branch of the tree and the sun was hot upon his back, for the leaves were few at this season of the year. He grew sleepier and sleepier as the arguments wound back over ground passed, or spun thinner and more delicately fanciful. Everyone of importance spoke once and many twice. When they had got rid of the first ideas, those shouted while the speakers were still panting with the haste of their coming, they were left with two notions of what to do with this awkward discovery of Opio's. The first was to get the cattle into bomas (it had mostly been done), arm, and wait to be attacked. The other was to leave the houses, assemble the whole clan and their herds in the crooked arm of a deep bend in the river and hope to escape discovery in the thick bush that grew there.

As each speaker called for one plan or the other there were shrill cries of approval or dissent from the women crowded about the circle of squatting men, for the whole clan listened to meetings of this importance. Opio heard the third round of speeches begin. In the end, as men, worn out by argument, allowed their turn to pass in silence, only the most stubborn and patient would last and force a decision. And then, in the pool of silence that followed the speech of a particularly tedious old man, Magere dropped a stone. He had listened silently to everything. Now he lifted his head and said, "Wait until it's dark and attack *them.*"

"Eh!"

"I said, wait until it's dark and *attack* them."

Everyone spoke at once.

"*Attack* them! Attack *Nandi!* The boy said there were thirty. *Thirty* devils! Maybe more. How can one guess what they're up to? Do nothing and perhaps they'll raid down the river to No's clan."

Magere stood up and made little marks in the dust with his toes until they were silent. Then he spoke for longer than anyone had ever heard him speak before, very calmly and simply. Many there felt themselves to be insulted by the way Magere spoke, as if he were explaining to small children and not land and cattle owners and the fathers of families.

"They aren't raiding," he said, "they've finished that. How else would they have cattle with them? The raid was last night, and far away too, for they were caught here by daylight returning. Why else should they be where they are? They won't attack, they're hiding. That means they're afraid. By now, unless they saw Opio, and he says they didn't, they'll believe themselves to be safe, and because they've driven cattle all night they'll be tired and sleep. They won't move until about two hours after sunset and then they'll make for the hills. Now, is what I've said true?"

The crowd shifted and muttered and considered.

Magere was known because he was a son of Okoth. But he was a younger son and still childless. In their world it is only what a man has done and has that counts, and

Magere had done and possessed little. He had made no important mark anywhere.

"Mm," they murmured. "Yes, yes, perhaps it's true but . . . but in that case we have only to wait until—"

"Of course it's true," shouted Magere, "and since it's true let's attack them at dark. They're Nandi. They'll not expect us. And do you know why? Because they're accustomed to Joluo running like rats every time a Nandi clears his throat. It's not a flattering thought, but since it's so let's profit by it. They don't know the ways among those stones, but we do. Every man of you played there as a child and could find the paths with his eyes closed."

The crowd clamored that it was better to wait.

Then, for the first time, they heard the harsh voice that was to change many of their lives. The veins swelled in Magere's throat and his eyes grew bloodshot.

"Are we lizards that creep up the wall into the thatch every time a woman drops a pot? When my father lived the young men were given spears and told to be ready to use them. Now they stay on the rafters and men . . . *men*" (the scorn in his voice made them shift uneasily) ". . . men keep their digging sticks sharp. You've babbled here for half a day as to whether you should hide under this bush or that. Now those of you who are men get your spears, if you've not forgotten where they lie. If ten of you are here armed an hour before sunset I'll show you how to teach the Nandi such a lesson that in future they'll run crying for their mothers when they so much as see a Joluo cow. Now *go,* and leave me to think how this shall be done."

And they went. Without further argument, for Magere was suddenly a man to be feared and obeyed. They went to their houses for spears, thoughtfully, many of them overthoughtfully, and these persuaded their wives to assure them that it was too late to go fighting Nandi. It was not so much that they were cowardly as that the idea was a new one and the Joluo people take a great deal of time to get used to a new idea.

When he was alone Magere stayed standing on the beaten earth of the meeting place. To Opio, still as a chameleon on his branch, his uncle seemed suddenly very huge, and lonely, and a little sad-looking. Then as Opio watched him a thought seemed to come to Magere, and he turned round and called softly: "Opio! Opio the Fish! Are you there?"

"I'm here," said Opio from the tree.

"Good," replied Magere. "We'll need you. Come down here now and tell me exactly where they were and what you saw."

So Opio scrambled down and sat in front of his uncle and answered questions. Over his story time and again he was led. Where were they? Where was the sun when he saw them? How many did he see? How did he count them and how long did he stay to count them? How were they armed? And none of them were watching? Could he be sure? Again and again the same questions in slightly different words and each time Opio thought more deeply about his answers.

Then they stopped and Magere seemed to stare at him absently for a while before forgetting him. He sat brooding and presently Opio crept away and curled up among the great bare roots of the tree and felt its bark warm and rough against his back. And after a long while men came one by one and squatted wordlessly before the silent Magere and waited.

When it was an hour to sunset he looked up and counted the few who were prepared to follow him. There were neighbor Ochieng and his two sons. The old herdsman Odongo and his eldest son Ochiel were there. So were nine men from the Oluoch family who lived up the river at the very edge of the settlement, a stubborn and quarrelsome lot whom few liked, but hardy and men to be reckoned with. Seven men came from the families who lived beyond the ford, led by a hale old man called Ogot, a cantankerous busybody who thought his words not sufficiently listened to in clan affairs, and who had come now for the reason he did almost everything, to spite the rest. There were, as well, three landless tenants who worked for richer men. They were hoping for loot.

Twenty-four, all armed with spears, and a few carried stained unlovely shields.

Magere counted them again.

"Twenty-four," he said.

Then he smiled with a sudden sweetness that took them by surprise, and they grinned back and felt bound together with a purpose and different and better than other men.

"Well," said Magere, "the fewer of us, the bigger share of cattle each. It's enough. Opio the Fish, come here and play the man better than most of your clan. Now, all of you, follow me."

And they did, going downstream to where the houses and the tilled land ended and the rocks and thorns began.

7

The rocks among which the Nandi were hidden stood on a small rise about a mile south of the river. They covered as much ground as three or four big farms and were the bones of a small hill, the soil of which had long since gone to the lake with endless ancient floods. The country round was flat and empty, lightly grown over with small thorn trees, but at one place a bow-shaped gully, an old bed of the river, curved near, and in and about this the trees were thicker and undergrown with clumps of aloes and euphorbia.

Magere's band went by way of this. The sun was down by the time they reached the place where Opio had last seen his flock that morning, but the sky was still light in the west and the rocks loomed up hugely against it. There were no signs of goats and sheep, no sound of Mbuzi's bell. Opio wondered what had happened to them and was faintly surprised that he could think calmly about a disaster so complete as the losing of all his flock.

Here, in the shelter of a clump of ojuok, tangled and thickened with the vines of wild gourds, they halted and gathered together in the shadows. Magere listened to Opio's whispered directions and then considered. He played with a plan of dividing his men and attacking the Nandi from two sides, but after a glance at them he abandoned the idea. They were huddled close, peering at the shadows with rolling eyes. Now, indeed, if a Nandi had cleared his throat they would have run. Only old Odongo looked as unconcerned as ever, and one of the Oluoch sons, an ugly ox of a man with broken protruding teeth, grinned and spat on his hands.

Magere made up his mind, looked at the dying light, decided it was late enough, and led on deeper among the rocks. Before doing so he arranged his force. He took with him Oketch, the Oluoch boy, and placed just behind the seven men who carried shields. The rest followed closely in whatever order pleased them.

It was that balanced moment when night and day change guard. A monkey on a branch, not yet quite asleep, chattered nervously as they went by. The bats of the rocks flew in clouds and the panting men could smell their leathery scent. An owl passed with a soft explosion of feathers that brought their hearts into their mouths.

Opio walked with his uncle, on his left to leave the man's spear side free. As it grew darker he held his hand. They crossed the meadow where he had searched for toadstools, crowded with shadows now and looking smaller, and left it by a cleft between two rocks, a gateway as black as the inside of a hut entered at noon. Then, two more grassy pools in the dusk beyond, there came from somewhere ahead the grumbling complaint of a cow as it got to its feet. They all heard it and stopped as one man. It was very close, the other side of a clifflike rock three times the height of a man. It came from where Opio had seen the Nandi that morning and he squeezed Magere's hand and whispered, "Yes."

Then before and above them, and there was still light enough in the sky to see, a man stood up. They held their breath and stared at him, a gaunt bony figure that raised its arms and stretched out the creases of the day's waiting. Opio thought that he heard the yawn and sigh. Then the shape bent and there was a faint clatter as a shield and spear were picked up, before it vanished, climbing down and beyond. As though it were being swallowed by the rock, jerkily, feet first. It was the sentry that Opio had missed that morning. He was unhurried and had seen nothing to alarm him.

Then Opio felt himself lifted by his uncle onto a high ledge and heard him whisper that he must stay there until fetched, and below the men pressed on, shadows swallowed by shadows.

Opio saw nothing of the battle but he heard it. The band went on round the rocks and there, as each explained to the others afterward, but never to another person, the fear that had sat on their backs left them like a bird taking flight. The Nandi were either asleep or in the muddle of first waking when Magere's twenty-four charged in with a yell. The cattle lurched to their feet, blaring, and stampeded, trampling sleeping men and separating them from weapons and comrades. The Nandi ran in every direction, convinced an army was upon them, each man keeping pace with his own fear, tripped by sprawling roots, bewildered in the cellars and alleys of that city of stones; at last no longer warriors, only hunted creatures anxious to hide.

Opio heard it all. He lay hugging the rock, which still held the day's sun within it, and he shivered with fright and excitement, while below the shouting, the thudding feet and plunging, screaming cattle spread everywhere. Hours later, it seemed, footsteps stopped below, and Magere's voice, hoarse and tired and full of triumph, said: "Opio! Opio the Fish! Where are you? Opio, are you still there?"

Then Opio gave a little gasp of relief and discovered that he could not speak, only slide stiffly down the rock and be caught and lifted to Magere's shoulder where he was carried for a space, then put down on a soft skin whose fine tickling hair was too long and silky for cow-skin. It smelt of soot and grease and something foreign, not of his people, and was, as he discovered next morning, a great colobus monkey-skin cloak, left by the Nandi.

And there, almost at once, he slept. And while he did so the hunt went on. What remained of the Nandi were sought out and killed. Most died among the rocks. Two were found next morning, hiding in grain pits a mile away. Three got clean away to the hills, where their people treated them harshly, for they had returned without cattle or comrades or even spears. Jackals, not men, their clan brothers shouted, and the women took up the cry. The elders heard their tale and then dismissed them contemptuously, and they found that life there was not to be endured and fled to the high cold forests and vanished from their tribe.

On Kano, Magere counted his men and only one was missing. It was a son of the Oluoch family and they found him the next morning, dead beside another dead man, who was, if they had known it, the leader Chelegat. That night they lit fires and gathered the cattle together slowly throughout the hours of darkness that remained, and also what loot in the way of spears and gear they came across. When it was light they searched better and found more. When they were certain they had all the beasts there were they kicked earth over the fires and drove the cattle back to the huts. They came home shouting with triumph, driving the weary, frightened cows.

On the way they met Opio's father, returning from his relatives in No.

Onyango stared at the men and cattle and then at Opio dancing in the dust behind.

"What are you doing?" he shouted. "And where's the flock?"

He had heard nothing of what had happened.

Opio stopped short in mid-leap. He had completely forgotten the flock.

"I don't know, Father," he stammered, and then without waiting for Onyango to say more he ran home trembling to find out.

"What in the name of Gogo is going on here?" shouted Onyango, but everyone was too excited to explain.

Opio ran panting to the cattle boma. The flock were

there, bleating to be let out. He counted them by eye. Every one. Mbuzi had brought them home the night before, on his own.

8

Two days later Magere divided the captured cattle among his followers. They had been grazed and watered with Onyango's cattle in the meantime, for which service Onyango had been paid a heifer. Now they were gathered in a rough boma of hastily cut thorns and the twenty-three survivors of the battle sat to one side, isolated by their glory. They did not, however, let this stand in the way of them keeping a sharp eye on their interests.

Opio sat on a nearby ant heap and enjoyed the battle of will and wits.

Those who had stayed at home when great deeds were being done looked on with envy and blamed their wives.

Magere divided, keeping, as was only right, a chief's share for himself.

It was a lengthy and by no means easy business. The cattle were all good, one hundred and eleven of them, several fine beasts for every man. But there were bulls and cows, heifers and grown calves, and they were red and black, white and straked. And each man had his fancies.

After some discussion Magere said that the division should be made by each man coming forward in turn to choose a beast and that when each had an equal number the rest should be added to his own share because he had led.

They considered this proposal for a long time. The trouble was that not one of them could divide one hundred and eleven by twenty-four (the dead man's share would go to his family) and know what number remained for Magere. In the end they gave grudging agreement, but it was a gamble whose result they were prepared to argue about when they could see more clearly what it was. This was not mentioned but fully understood by all there.

Then they debated in what order they should make the choice, and about this words flew thick and fast, for the best beasts stood out plainly and everyone hungered for possession of them, and tried to avoid looking at his heart's desire in case his companion followed his eyes and got there first out of plain spite.

Odongo found the way out of this problem.

"Let Magere choose first," he proposed, "for he led and it's his right. But let each of us put some small thing of his own into a great pot and then shall Magere take them out with his eyes lifted to the sky. In the order his hand blindly chooses so shall the owners of the things take the beasts."

So it was decided to follow this course and a great waterpot was fetched from the nearest house and each thrust in whatever he chose among his small possessions: snuff-gourds, a feather, a stone, a tooth-stick, a charm, a beaded fringe, the stone from a cow's stomach (worn as an amulet), a wooden comb; every man found something that could be sworn to by those who knew him as being his, and his alone. Oluoch put in two things, one for his dead son.

"And what are *you* putting in, Opio?" asked Magere.

Opio got uncertainly to his feet.

"No!" shouted old Oluoch, smashing his fist down on his thigh. "No, I say! He's but a boy. A child too young to carry a spear. He gets nothing."

Magere turned and glowered at him.

"Oluoch," he said, "he found the cattle and brought the warning. He led us to the place and led us well. Without him there wouldn't have been anything to divide. He takes his share with the rest."

Oluoch got to his feet, a grim, ugly old man, hard as leather and stubborn as he was greedy. His sons bunched muttering behind him.

"Aye," he said, "he gets his share and that way your family takes double share over and above what you take as leader. He's a child and I don't share with a child."

"And I say you do with this one!" shouted Magere in a passion, and his neck swelled and he looked as terrible as he had done before in the council, and Oluoch was put down by the nakedness of Magere's anger.

Magere turned back to Opio.

"I asked what you were putting in as your token, Opio," he said.

"But I haven't anything," replied Opio. "Nothing!" And he flapped his arms, and indeed it was plain that he had nothing, and his naked lean little body twisted with embarrassment.

"Then let him put in nothing," said neighbor Ochieng placidly. "He'll choose each time after all of us, since, as Oluoch says, he's but a child. Though it's right he should choose too, since, as Magere says, he's a bold one and might make a man."

At this, those who felt Opio too young to be favored, and did not like to say so, felt a little mollified. Ochieng was always a peacemaker. Opio noted, however, that Oluoch still looked at him with hatred, and he decided that here, at least, was one old man whose path it would be best to avoid in the future.

At this moment a busybody of a man called Otsieno, one of the onlookers who had taken no part in the battle, could no longer bear his envy in silence. First making an important noise in his throat, he ventured to point out, in a voice that all could hear, that the cows were, as a matter of plain fact, not Magere's to divide. They belonged, he said, to someone or other of their tribe who had been robbed of them by the Nandi.

Having said this, he scratched an ear delicately and looked round for support. He seemed to have some among those who could expect no cattle.

Magere turned to deal with Otsieno.

"We took the cows from the Nandi and they took them from someone else. Is that what you're saying?"

"Yes, indeed," replied Otsieno. "That's what we're telling you."

Oluoch shifted his glare from Opio and turned it on this new threat to his winnings, and his sons swung with him.

"Well," said Magere judicially, "it's said that he who has the cow drinks the milk, and we certainly have the cows and it would be said by some that we've earned them. When in the past the Nandi stole cattle I never heard much argument as to whom they belonged to then. I mind that you lost seven last year, Otsieno. Tell me, did you go and claim them back?"

"That's not the same thing at all," protested Otsieno. "Certainly I lost seven last year. The Nandi stole them, but no matter who *has* them they *belong* to me. Isn't that right, friends?"

"Yes," murmured the crowd, looking wistfully at the fine lakeside cattle. "Yes, that's certainly so."

"They belong to you, then, and the Nandi just look after them for you? Is that what you're saying?"

Otsieno considered the point.

"Yes," he declared at last. "In a sense that's so."

"Good," said Magere, smacking the flank of the finest of the bulls. "Then we'll look after these for the Nandi and anyone else who thinks he used to own them, and—tell you what, Otsieno—I'll give them back when you ask the Nandi to return yours."

At that there was a snicker of laughter from the crowd, for Otsieno was not widely known for his courage. Magere turned again to the division of the cattle and Otsieno left quietly, for it was something that he did not feel he could bear to watch.

That night Opio shut the boma gate on his father's cattle and four beasts of his own. His heart was full and he felt himself to be the richest boy in Kano. Which, since in the hearts of his people cattle were the only real wealth, he might well have been.

A month later the clan from which the cattle had been stolen heard rumors of what had happened to them and they sent a party of men to find out where they were, and, if possible, to claim them back.

When they had explained their errand to the elders of Okoth's clan these nodded and sent for Magere. When he came the spokesman for the lakeside people told his tale again. "And that's what we heard had happened," he said in finishing.

"It's been greatly exaggerated," commented Magere.

The spokesman stared at him stonily. He knew. Then he turned again to the elders.

"We want our cattle back," he said flatly.

"I know of no cattle of the kind you describe," replied one elder.

"It's unlikely they'd be here," added another. "We're peaceful folk and such a feat as you've described wouldn't be like us at all."

"If, as you say, the Nandi took them," said the third, "then the best place to look for them would be *there*." And he pointed an arm carelessly to the wall of hills across the plain.

"If you dare," whispered Magere. A whisper that could just be heard.

The lakeside people smiled bitterly, thanked them for their hospitality and went home.

A week later Magere slaughtered a cow and feasted a number of elders.

9

Magere had said that the Nandi would be taught a lesson that would keep them from Joluo cattle. But nobody believed that, least of all Magere. That was not at all like the Nandi. However, everyone wished it to be so, and, as the days slipped peacefully past, they forgot about the matter for most of the time. Only occasionally did a man's eyes rest on a smear of smoke from a distant cooking fire in the hills and wonder what mischief was being hatched there.

And for a month nothing did happen.

Then one morning there came down to the plain a wrinkled old man dressed in a black-and-white cloak of colobus fur. High on the far slopes the white of his flapping garment caught the eye and the herdboys saw him at first light and brought the news to their elders. He came slowly, so that it was well into the morning before they could see him clearly, hopping over the rocks like a crow catching flying ants. It was clear he was both old and alone, and they were not alarmed, only curious.

By the time he reached the cotton tree all the old men of the clan were seated there on stools and hundreds of the people stood round them in a half-circle. The children peered between their betters' legs or perched high on the branches to watch.

The old Nandi was weary from his journey, the heat and his heavy robes, or perhaps it was just his great age. He used a short hunting spear as a stick and he leaned heavily on it as he walked, and the red dust of the plain lay in the wrinkles of his face. He stopped when he reached the tree, looked round him at the silent people, murmured a greeting, laid his spear down carefully on the ground and squatted beside it.

After a little while, at a sign from one of the elders, a woman brought a half-gourd filled with good water, cool from the depths of a hut, and the Nandi accepted it. He rinsed his mouth out and spat, took two or three tiny sips, poured out what remained onto the ground, and returned the woman her gourd with a single gentle word of thanks. Then while they watched him with deep interest he fumbled clumsily beneath his skins and brought out a beautifully beaded snuff bottle made from red cowhide. Many a man there coveted that snuff bottle and it held their eyes as he shook out a careful measure of the black powder into a clawlike hand. He snuffed vigorously and sneezed twice. Everyone jumped a little at the first, a thin sound, like the sneeze of a chicken. Then they waited anxiously for the second. When at last it came, and was enjoyed and done with, he sighed, stowed the bottle carefully away, climbed stiffly to his feet, muttered a farewell and set off home across the plain. An hour later the black-and-white cloak was still visible, toiling up the hillside, tiny with distance.

But the circle of elders had lost interest in him.

They were looking at what he had left behind—a hunting spear lying on the dusty floor of the council place, polished blade pointing toward them.

The Nandi had announced that they intended war.

10

So it had to be war with the Nandi. No longer a bagatelle of young men raiding, stealing a cow by stealth and laughing at last at the risks when they were safe away and their hearts stopped thumping. Not that, but war. Tribe against tribe in broad daylight, and if they won they would take the land, perhaps, and anything else that came to their greedy hands, and the survivors could begin life again, somewhere else. Up in those hills they knew that the cunning old men who ruled the Nandi had sat in council and made their choice and sent one of their number with the spear. In their own time they would send others running with their orders, young men this time, and the warriors would obey without question and come out armed and painted for war. Gladly, for they had a disgrace to wipe off the record.

In a sense it was a compliment, for the Nandi only made war in this fashion upon people whom they considered to be in some sort their equals. They had never thought the Joluo to be this before. It was a compliment that many of Magere's people could have endured to have done without.

The council made Magere their war leader. He was the only man who had ever worsted the Nandi, and also, as one sour old man put it: "You brought this trouble on us with your rashness. Now get us out of it."

Magere, not at all insulted, rose up, squared his great shoulders (he seemed to have grown in size as well as reputation since that night's business among the rocks), made his plans and gave his orders. They were obeyed. The clan had wrangled through the whole of a long hot day over what should be done about what almost all of them believed to be a disaster. But having made a decision and named a leader they argued no longer and did as they were told. That was their Joluo way. Magere would be followed so long as he was successful and until the danger was past.

He acted vigorously. Command came naturally to him, as if in the manner born, though no one had ever noticed the gift in him before. And as the people obeyed many of them marveled, for what they did seemed the obvious course to follow, yet they only discovered it when he had spoken.

First someone with sense (it was Ochieng) was sent to their kinsmen at No to ask for help. The elders of No listened to his tale and then sent him away while they deliberated. When he was recalled the next day they said this:

"We want to help. But the planting season is on us and

if our young men go before the ground is broken and sown, then later we'll starve. So you must wait. When we've dug and sown we'll come."

Ochieng had to be content with this, but when he returned with the message Magere seemed satisfied enough.

"It'll do," he said. "The Nandi won't come until their own fields have been planted and that won't happen until the first rain has fallen. Let's hope the people of No do their business quickly and don't haggle too long afterward."

Then he set his own folk to work.

The fields were broken early that year, while the land was still dry. It was heart-breaking work and every soul who was not wanted elsewhere labored at pounding the iron-hard clods to fragments so that it should be done quickly. While they did so all the cattle and flocks were branded with their owners' marks and driven south of the river in several big herds, as far as possible from the Nandi. The pasture they fed on belonged to the No clan, but their kinsmen gave them the right. They were put in the charge of the older children and a few elderly men too stiff and frail for fighting. A few goats were kept back for milk and some sheep for meat. Opio was among the children who were sent with the cattle.

Then a dozen young men were sent to keep watch along the foothills. When Magere explained their task to them he said this: "Don't wait to tell me when you see them coming. I want the news when one hour or day so much as *smells* differently from the last. I want it when a fire burns at night where it didn't burn before, when grazing buck lift their heads more often than usual, when a rhino makes a new path down the hill to water, when kites gather on the hilltops."

The young men listened carefully and then went, carrying their spears and bags of corncake. They lived in thorn shelters and watched the buck paths leading down from the heights and the distant fires of the Nandi at night. They kept their eyes and ears open and tried to judge the moment of which Magere had spoken. Odongo's son, Ochiel, was among them and also Oketch, that son of Oluoch who had grinned and spat on his hands before the Battle Among the Rocks. Magere remembered men and the signs that showed what they were made of.

When the first heavy shower of the year fell the seed was put into the ground hastily and it was hoped that the rain was not a false promise and the sowing have to be done again, as sometimes happened. It was thought, however, to be fairly safe, for the hills Kisii way were clear and black-edged and seemed to have moved nearer, and that was always reckoned to be a good sign. After this the women and the old men and the rest of the children joined those who had gone with the cattle and only the young men were left to cook their own beans and millet and watch the hills and wait.

They had now done everything they could. The oxhide shields had been fetched out, their wooden frames searched, tested and repaired where necessary. Then they were soaked for the night in the river and left next day in the sun, so that the hide shrank drum-tight over the wood and dried hard and tough as iron. Spears and simis were ground sharp on the wet rocks of the river bed, and the furbishings of war—the ostrich plumes, long cow-tail girdles, platted thongs and hide anklets—were put where they could be snatched up at need.

The homesteads were empty silent places without children's cries, women's chatter or the sounds of cattle. The men remaining were silent and idle and on edge.

"When will they come?" they asked, and Magere replied:

"After the first millet has been planted in the hills. After that a little space for men to gather and sacrifices to be made. Then they'll come. Soon now. And they'll go back faster than they came."

One morning the men of No arrived, more than a hundred and forty young men painted and armed, eager and boasting of what they would do. So they had not forgotten, and all hearts were lifted by their arrival. Sheep were slaughtered to feast them and men moved over and slept more crowded in the huts at night. Some of the No men joined the scouts in the foothills to stop gaps in the line and make warning more certain.

Their kinsmen's war party was led by an elderly man called Ramula and he gladly gave Magere the first place.

"One must lead if there's not to be confusion," he said, straight out, "and it had best be you, for you've fought Nandi and I haven't."

Magere thought that the elders of No must have chosen Ramula because he was unambitious and unlikely to cause trouble and he was silently thankful for their sense and treated him with great consideration and deference. He discussed all his plans with him before saying a word of them to any other man, and they shared the same house.

One other small event occurred at this time, and this was that Opio joined his uncle. He had been told to go with the women and help herd the cattle and had done so. But after a week he had run away, back to Magere. For this he was promptly beaten and told to return to his work.

"Off with you!" bellowed Magere. "In war men and boys must do as they're told. Back to the cattle, brat. And stay there."

To Opio this was a new and frightening uncle and he had slunk off with his tail well between his legs. When he arrived, his father, who was too old for battle, had cuffed him heartily, and Grandmother Adero had spoken to him in a voice that might possibly have been heard by the Nandi themselves. So he had wept and sulked and joined the other boys with the cattle, but in two days he had returned to the settlement by stealth and was found skulking in a half-filled granary.

When he was led in by the ear, Magere had laughed and let him alone.

"Stay then," he shouted, "and if the Nandi don't eat you perhaps you'll bring us the same good luck you did last time."

So Opio, glad to get out of the granary, where the year-old cobs had made a most hard and nobbly bed, and even more pleased not to be beaten again, had tried to make himself useful. He had fetched water from the river, gathered firewood and blown the fire awake, watched the porridge bubbling, and not cared at all that this was usually the work of women.

And at last he had seen the Nandi army come down from the hills to Kano Plain.

11

The scouts did well.

Nightly they had seen the fires increase on the group of hills called Soina. Also they had observed kites and vultures circling there by day and they guessed that beasts were being slaughtered to feed a great company of men. They had sent word of both these signs to Magere as soon as they became certain there was no mistake, and so readiness had been ground to a fine edge.

Then, early one morning, they saw the Nandi, a black flood of men finding its way down the hill. Like water overflowing a bank and taking a new path, quickly where the way lay open, checking at an obstacle, winding round, but always coming on.

The scouts sent three of their number running like buck over the plain and whistled in those who watched to their flanks. Then they kicked over the rough sleeping shelters, gathered their gear and fell back slowly toward the river, watching the Nandi as they went. These came on with no attempt at concealment and without hurry, and the scouts retreated as leisurely, lying behind thorn bushes to count heads, until they came near and it was time to move again.

Behind them from the houses the Joluo went to their places, silent and serious. Men took the earth colors, red and black and white, and painted their chests and faces with the stripes and blotches that meant war. They tightened thongs that bound ostrich plumes to their heads, for these would give them the height and frightfulness that might check an enemy's courage. They took shields and spears and ran from the huts across the fields through gaps in the sisal hedges and stood in a great double line where the cultivated land finished. They edged together closely and felt the comfort of men to either side. Then they rested the spears and heavy shields on the ground, adjusted hide anklets and headdresses, squatted on their hams, and watched the enemy coming closer.

The Nandi came down like a great herd of cattle running to the water when the land is dry. Plumes of long hair waved like papyrus feathers in the wind, and the whole hillside, usually so still and empty, became alive and threatening.

At the foot, where the ground flattened and the rocks and scrub thinned, they made a long line and advanced as if they were dancing. The Joluo could see them stamp their feet together, in time, but so gently that not a sound was to be heard. Later, when they came nearer, they could feel the sound running through the ground. Every few running paces a check, and then a gentle stamp, and at each stamp the spears were lifted and twisted so that the bright blades glittered in men's eyes like sunlight glancing on water.

They moved like this through the young grass, for with the first few showers it was springing fresh and green. Where trees stood in their way the line opened and then healed and the trees stood now behind it. When they reached the outlying fields they halted. Close now, and Opio, flat on his stomach behind a hedge, could see the Nandi witch doctors in their heavy cloaks, clumsy like gorged vultures, running along the ranks and dropping their heavy ironwood staffs on the feet of those who ran out of line. The young men were obedient and their faces showed no pain and they did not so much as glance at the man who struck the blow. They hung forward, eager as dogs, and panted.

The Joluo got to their feet, edged closer to each other, hefted their spears to find the balancing point, brought the great shields up and licked dry lips. In all some six or seven hundred men were gathered there and no sound to be heard.

The Nandi began to sing, not one of them more than whispering the words, but the whole a gentle murmuring that rose and fell and filled the world with sound. It did not seem a noise made by men, but something natural, the wind in the grass or water falling through stones, and although the men who sang still made no movement forward their feet quietly beat out the time.

"Shake out, shake out our line,
Tread to the right, brother,
Give my spear room.
Are the war-bags full?
Brimming and stamped down hard.
Are the spears sharp?
They cut like knife grass.
When we left the houses this morning,
Did the honey bird, the bird of war,
Sing to the right hand or the left?
It sang to the right.
Good. Has the spear been sent ahead?
It was sent.
Shake out, shake out our line,
Tread to the right, brother,
Give my spear room.
So.
Is it time to begin?
BEGIN!"

Then the shields were tossed and the spears came up like bared teeth and the Nandi screamed as they swept forward, and seven hundred ordered men became a heaving, swaying mob, shouting and cursing, and the spears stabbed and stabbed.

There were no lines now. They shattered and groups of men danced and feinted, peered with glittering eyes over shield edges at men who did the same before them. No man saw the whole battle, only his own private battle.

Perhaps it lasted the time it takes for a hungry man to

still his appetite, but in that little time spears and shields grew as heavy as stone, men panted as if they had run all day in the heat and the world swung before their eyes in a mist of exhaustion.

And then the Nandi broke.

Both peoples were equal in numbers and muscle and courage, but the Joluo had a stubbornness with their strength that was very hard to overcome. Men call them slow-witted, and perhaps it is true, but everything that day was very simple to understand and they did so. It was daylight and cool with the coming rain and their homes spread round them, the first blades of corn beginning to show in the dug earth and the cooking fires still smoking outside the huts. It would all be taken away and before them were the men who had come to do it.

They gathered failing strength and went on a little longer than they knew it was possible to endure.

And they were led. Magere led them. Like an angry ox. Like a rock from which spears seemed to rebound.

The Nandi gave slowly at first, then quicker, then scattered and fled. Groups of their warriors, turned in the confusion so that they faced the way they had come, took panic, fled toward the river, were lost among the great hedges about the homestead, were hunted and killed. Those that kept their wits and their feet ran back to the hills. The rest stayed where they had fallen and the kites and vultures which had gathered all day over the place swept lower as it became deserted, plummeted to the ground and suddenly, without grace, began to move in the grass with clumsy strutting gait.

The Joluo felt the excitement die in them, felt a weariness like death in all their limbs, knew life to be sad and flat. They rested, panting, and then began to recognize and mourn their dead.

The battle was over.

Late that afternoon Magere, by simple stubbornness, gathered the youngest and boldest of his men. He did it by bribery and argument and anger and blows. He led them that night up the paths to the hills and they groaned as they climbed and cursed this leader who laid tasks upon their backs beyond the strength of men to endure. And Magere grinned back and cursed them and hounded them on.

In the morning they flooded into the Nandi villages at the top. They burned houses and scattered the warriors who rested there, tired and hungry men, chopfallen with defeat. It was a stroke they had never dreamed the Joluo could make. They judged falsely from their own weariness and despair.

The Joluo gathered so many cattle that the party was hard pressed to drive them. They brought them at last to the plain, men stumbling with weariness, too tired to feel triumph.

Magere had spoken the truth. The Nandi had returned faster than they came. Some of them.

12

The Battle of Kano made Magere not only the war leader of his clan but of his people also. He became no longer content merely to farm his land and keep his hedge mended as a good Joluo should. Instead, every year after the harvest he grew restless. Then the shields were brought down from the rafters and cared for, the spears ground to an edge that made the testing thumbs wary as they ran over them. The women half cooked the millet flour and beat it down hard in the leather bags with the blunt ends of grinding pestles.

And his men gathered.

They came at first from the people he knew, from his own clan and neighboring No. But as his fame spread they came from Asembo and Nyakatch, from the marshes of Uyoma and the islands of Rusinga, from distant Gem and Sakwa beside the lake. From wherever Dholuo was spoken and the name of Magere was known men came. And what men! The good farmers of Kano were wary and uncomfortable when they met them and kept a close eye on their daughters and their stock, for these were rootless, landless men, vague as to their clan and family, hot-eyed and in their faces something of the hyena's famished grin.

From men like these Magere made up his war parties and raided the neighboring tribes, the Kisii, Nandi, the

Kipsigis, Maragoli and even the faraway Masai of the wide grass steppes to the south. As Opio grew to be a man he saw them set off yearly, watching from an ant heap beyond the fields until the dancing ostrich plumes could no longer be seen for the haze rising from the plain. And he saw them return, weeks, sometimes months, later, driving captured cattle, carrying looted spears with odd-shaped blades, skins of soft strange fur, beads and heavy copper bracelets. Then the women screamed the strange warbling cries kept for welcoming men from war and the long nights were full of wild dancing and boasting songs.

"He who stones the hive must not complain if the bees wake angry."

These raids drew raids in return. Even the Masai sent warriors along the lake shore where they had never come before, men whose hair was dressed with oil and red earth, with faces which seemed carved from polished brown wood, carrying spears with blades a yard long. They came and others too and great battles were fought. But then it was not only the hungry men who followed Magere but also the solid farmers, for their lands and cattle were in danger.

Far and wide now men spoke in a new way about the Joluo. By the great cattle tribes they had been regarded as soil-scratchers, people who hung on to any earth they infected, as difficult to dislodge as ticks on a cow's udder, men only because they were forked with legs. Now it seemed that the creatures could fight.

The Nandi, Kipsigis and Masai licked their wounds and marveled at the change.

The legend began round the fires where men talked together about past battles and showed old scars. It gathered force in the songs invented to make those deeds memorable. As the years passed the story was added to until it became a belief held by all—a certainty.

It was said that Magere was different from other men. He was like a stone. Not just in a manner of speaking, as it might be said that one was lionhearted and another swift as lightning. No, he was stonelike. Flying spears struck him and fell useless with their points turned and blunted while Magere would laugh and go on unharmed.

Even his enemies believed it. All the people he fought, even the shy Teriki from the Maragoli Hills, who hunt with poisoned arrows in the forest and deal with devils, they knew that he could not be killed in battle. And, with the rest, they edged away to try their luck on men with more humanity to them.

In the end no man would fight him by choice.

They called him Magere the Stone.

Opio

1

For Opio it was a troublesome time. Sometimes he felt himself to be a man, at others still a boy.

That year Magere went raiding the Kisii.

They had been moving down from their hills into Kano. Not in great numbers—they were not sure enough of themselves for that—but small clan groups were edging their homes down along the southern streams that ran into the plain, and breaking new fields on what was felt to be Joluo land. It was true that nobody lived there as yet, but boundary marks of wild sisal had been planted, and to the Joluo, it was waiting for their sons.

Also the Kisii had been active after their neighbors' cattle in a somewhat timid fashion and it was felt that they deserved a lesson.

Magere did not take a large party, only sixty men in all. They went south early in the year and expected to be away a month.

Opio had begged to be allowed to go with them, but Magere had replied that he was, as yet, too young.

"Another year and I'll take you," he said. "Stay at home now and help your father and mother. They're growing old and need you."

"They'll be even older next year," protested Opio reasonably enough.

But Magere would not budge from his decision and the party went without Opio.

It went also without others who longed for a chance to earn a few cattle with their spears. There were many who were disappointed about this and the noisiest of these over it was the man called Oketch, son of that same Oluoch who had quarreled with Magere over Opio's share of cattle. Oketch was more often called the Boar, and he had been given this name because his teeth protruded from his lips like tusks.

"One would think Magere to be the only fighting man in the clan from the way some talk," grumbled the Boar. "Yet others have done as well. I was there among the Rocks and in the Great Battle too, not to mention a dozen raids since. I tell you the Boar has seen a little fighting and a man could earn cattle under my direction as well as he could under another. Perhaps better."

Here he sucked his teeth and glowered round to see if anyone wished to dispute about it. No one did, for the Boar was strong and unpleasant to cross. Opio knew that it was just this loud-mouthed desire to lead and love of argument which had made Magere not ask him to come, for all that he was better than most men in a fight. Opio had heard his uncle say so.

However, the upshot of it was that the Boar began to plan a raid of his own and other men who had been disappointed by Magere said that they would go with him. Among them was Opio.

He hesitated for a day or so before asking. Then one long afternoon he could bear his idleness no longer and he ran to the Boar and asked if he could go also and, somewhat to Opio's surprise, he was welcomed. Long after it was all over he realized that a young and untried nephew of Magere had only been accepted because it gave the Boar a feeling that he was scoring by doing so. But Opio did not see it in this way at the time because he had not yet grown a nose for a man's motives.

Ten others came as well as Opio, all good salted warriors except one. There were three more Oluoch brothers, Ogalo, Kasuku and Omondi, and with them came two of Oluoch's tenants, good enough men but for some reason considered to be unlucky. Also a man called Ombok, whom Magere would certainly have taken had he not been from home at the time looking for a wife in Gem. He'd returned too late with no wife, only a newly healed scar on his head and a long tale of misunderstanding which no one fully understood. Then a pair called Ochuodo and Omolo joined. They were men from No who were living away from home until a quarrel with their clan had blown over. The last to get a place was a man named Odhiambo and he was only a little older than Opio and as untried. His family were rich, but none of them had any kind of reputation. Odhiambo was a big strong lad who always looked sleepy. He had been greatly tormented as a child by other children because of the number and variety of his fears, and why he wished to come at all was a mystery, because although he was strong he was comfort-loving and soft. The rumor went that the Boar took him because he had been paid a cow to do so.

They started a week after Magere had left for Kisii and at first they moved in his tracks. Then they turned west to the lake shore and followed this toward Masai country. For three days they were among their own people and were welcomed and fed. After that the war-bags had to be opened at night, though they did manage to spear some fish in the lake and this helped save the food. At night now they made thorn bomas and kept fires burning, for this was country that the reputation of the Masai kept empty and there were lions which could be heard through the darkness coming down to the water to drink.

They pushed on south. None of them had been this way before. The Oluoch brothers had raided in Masai, but they had gone by way of the Kisii Hills, descending their southern slopes to the steppe. Still they trusted to the lake for guide, for it was well known that the western border of Masai was the water and so sooner or later this road must take them there. But they found it to be no easy route and sometimes it was difficult to judge where the lake lay because of great marshes at its edge, fields of reeds and papyrus stretching mile after mile, with the wind chasing shadows across them. The reed flowers stretched above their heads and the roots stood in mud. It was hard to make or find a way through and much time was wasted going round. The birds they saw were their best guides. Skeins of duck pointed lakeward at evening; so did clumsy herons and heavy flying ibis. And by day the high-sailing fish eagles were, they knew, quartering open water invisible to a man sweating among the reeds.

When they did see the lake, for sometimes open country ran to it, the sands of its shore were black and glittered in the sun. In parts it was grown over with broken-backed-looking trees whose branches rooted again where they touched ground. A dismal place, which seemed peopled only by crocodiles. They lay like stranded canoes on the sand and watched the men passing with evil unwinking eyes.

Grumbling began. They had been from home half a month now and done nothing that brought any profit. Quarrels blew up over food and tasks and the party divided into two camps which bickered. On one side was the Boar, his three brothers and the two tenants, on the other Ombok, Ochuodo and Omolo. One night there was a fight between Ombok and Oluoch tenant over the sharing of some stale honey found in a dead tree, and for a while it seemed as if the two factions would fight it out with spears. Then the Boar showed sense and put a stop to it, for he saw that this path would lead to his losing men to command. So the quarrel was patched up.

Opio took no part in this or other quarrels. He found he disliked most of his companions and out of a need to talk to someone he found himself often with Odhiambo, who had suffered greatly during the march. He was clumsy and careless and always meeting small misfortunes which were either painful or ridiculous. He was bitten by a scorpion and lay groaning half a night; he walked into a troop of soldier ants and fled yelping, dropping load, weapons and even his skin kilt the better to pick the furious biting creatures off his body. The rest roared with laughter at his antics. And once he stepped into a patch of bog and sank at once to his waist. There he wallowed, unable to escape, whimpering for help, and the others laughed and jeered at his terror. Indeed it went on too long and if Ombok and Opio had not gone to his aid he would have drowned in mud, for it was up to his shoulders before they were permitted to let him take hold of a spear. Even then they were hard put to it to free him. The Boar and his cronies would do nothing to help.

So Odhiambo became the butt of the party and in a way it helped to keep them together, for tormenting Odhiambo gave most of them occupation. All indeed except Opio, who pitied the man and talked to him at night when they rested, and found him to be kind-hearted enough, but somewhat of a fool.

One good day they left the marshes. The lake curved away to the west, for all this time they had been following the gulf which ran into Kano. Now the shore doubled back toward the main lake and before them was open dry plain dotted with low thorns and deep in sun-bleached grass. Gullies, scooped out by floodwater, ran everywhere. This was Masai country and the grass that fed their herds stretched to the sky.

Almost at once they saw cattle, a small herd far off on the steppe. They left behind the skins they slept under at night, and the food-bags (almost empty now) and the shields, and with spears and simis crept nearer along the water gullies. It was easy to approach unseen and at last they all lay hidden in a hollow a stone's throw away.

The beasts fed peacefully. One of the herdsmen slept in the shadow of an ant heap, the other stood like a stork on one leg, leaning on a tall spear. He was dressed in a single skin tied over one shoulder, and his hair, red with mud and fat, was shaped like a helmet. The sleeping man lay with his neck upon a wooden rest to preserve the beauty of his sculptured hair. Their skins shone red in the sunlight. They were Masai.

The Joluo crouched close together along the edge of the hollow and waited to hear what the Boar would say they were to do.

Oketch looked at his waiting men and then his eye paused on Odhiambo and he grinned evilly and licked his jutting teeth.

"Odhiambo," he said quietly, "you're a promising young man but have yet to make your mark. Here's your chance. Go out and kill that man and get a heifer. A slab of meat would go down well tonight with our grain cake."

Odhiambo stared at him. Then he looked at the drifting cattle and the tall Masai with the long leaf-bladed spear. He looked for a long time and Opio, who was next to him, could see the blood beating in his throat.

"Go on, Odhiambo," whispered Oketch softly, "or can it be that you're afraid?"

Odhiambo gave a wild glance round. Then he made as if to rise, but when his shoulders were just off the ground he sank again and covered his face.

"Or are you afraid?" asked Oketch again.

Odhiambo moved his head violently but stayed down. Presently his shoulders began to shake and Opio heard him sob.

The Joluo looked on in silence.

Oketch turned to Opio.

"Opio," he said, "I'll kill the herdsman since it seems that Odhiambo feels unwell. Will you make a name for yourself with the other, or shall I give the work to someone who isn't a nephew of Magere the Stone?"

Opio saw his lips curl when he said Magere's name and he wondered why his uncle should be either greatly loved or equally hated but never anything less.

"It's as you wish, Oketch," said Opio.

"Good," said Oketch. "Now you should move first, Opio. After all, you come from a family of leaders."

Then Opio took his spear, feeling for the balance. He got to his knees and set his eyes on the sleeping herdsman. He judged the distance to be some sixty running paces. Then he breathed deeply, bounded to his feet and began to run. His last thought was a question as to whether Oketch would come as well or if he meant him to be killed. Then it did not seem to matter what Oketch did or intended, and he ran silently and swiftly.

The man with the cattle heard him when the distance was half covered. He turned and exclaimed, then yelled to his companion. Opio kept his eyes on his own man, saw him get to his knees, see the danger and then come to his feet with one lithe twist. To one side Opio saw the herdsman with the cattle bound toward him, spear up, then check and his attention go beyond Opio. So Oketch had come, after all, and he felt warmer toward that ugly, bitter one. Then he turned all his mind on the man he was trying to kill.

The Masai grabbed for his spear on the ground, missed, found it to be late and Opio near, drew a simi from inside his cloak in one graceful movement and twisted down and under Opio's spear thrust. He moved like an animal, effortless, feet dancing, sword sweeping up. Opio saw the return thrust coming, knew himself to be too late to avoid it, half turned . . . and then the Masai tripped on his wooden neck rest, the catlike grace crumbled and Opio's spear took him in the throat.

Opio turned, panting. The other Masai was dead, with Oketch standing over him. The Joluo swarmed up babbling from the hollow. The cows stared curiously at the newcomers and the nearest heifer snorted and ran plunging for a few paces. Then she calmed and after a while lowered her head to graze.

"It was well done, Opio," said Oketch, "but that Masai was a little unlucky, I thought."

Then he stared round him, missed Odhiambo and walked back to the hollow. Odhiambo still lay on his face. Oketch stood looking down at him for a moment and then he took the man's spear and put it across his knee. The shaft was made of tough white olive and Oketch struggled with it for a while with sweat on his face, but in the end it twisted and broke and he threw the pieces away.

Then he kicked Odhiambo.

He went on until Odhiambo got up, a hulking bull of a man, shoulders fallen forward, head hanging. He stood there trembling and said nothing.

"I see that I've brought a woman raiding, *A*dhiambo," said Oketch, and his voice leaned heavily on the female vowel of the altered name. "I wouldn't have chosen to do that but I can see a number of advantages for the future. At least there'll be someone to cook for us. Also to fetch the water. And you can carry the food-bags, *A*dhiambo the Coward."

And Adhiambo the Coward he became.

2

They turned back toward home, but not by the road they had come. Instead they cut inland, first finding and then skirting the Kisii Hills. It was dangerous because that way they might fall in with the Kisii in force, who would be pleased to gain a small but useful herd. Also, although they had no way of knowing how things had gone with Magere, it was possible that the Kisii might be smarting a little and anxious to get their own back on any Joluo they found. But Oketch took the risk because he had to. There would be grass for the cattle below the hills and they could not be taken through the swamps. The party moved very slowly now, out of a need for caution but also because of the beasts. A great deal of time had to be taken each day in grazing and watering them and this could not be hurried if they were to be kept in condition.

Adhiambo the Coward followed, carrying the food-bags. These were heavy again, filled with hastily dried meat. They had slaughtered a heifer the first night and feasted full. Adhiambo had sat silently apart and they had flung him scraps. They cut what meat could be carried and spread it on rocks to dry whenever they halted. All were more cheerful and united now because they were going home, because the raid had been a success and because Adhiambo gave them endless amusement. He was not only Adhiambo the Coward, he was also Adhiambo the Slave. Each day when they camped he cut the wood, searched for and drew water, lit a fire and cooked the meat. Also he did any other task that was demanded. His life was a hell of work and insult.

They called to him in high womanish voices:

"Adhiambo! Adhiambo, is the food ready yet?"

He scarcely spoke, only worked and did as he was told, took kicks and cuffs and mockery without complaint and, when he was allowed to rest, sat apart, hunched and silent. Once in the night, Opio heard him sobbing.

Opio did not mock him. He despised the man because his cowardice had been plain, but he thought that the blame for it could have been shared a little elsewhere.

After more than a week of steady monotonous droving

they rounded the great shoulder of the Kisii Highlands and camped that night beneath a red cliff. There was a cave at the bottom, a narrow crack in the rock, whose sides met in a pointed arch high above their heads. Inside it was dry, and although there were signs that an animal had lived there, probably a leopard, the traces were old and the place was a good shelter.

There was a stream below the cave and good grazing on either side of it. It was Opio's turn to watch the cattle and after watering them and drinking himself he let them feed beside the stream and sat on the bank to watch. The others went into the cave, except for Adhiambo, who wandered listlessly outside gathering firewood.

The cattle were soon satisfied and began to huddle together and lie down. They had grazed earlier that afternoon and were not hungry. When they were settled Opio knew that they would not move and he laid down his spear and shield, slipped off his kilt and lowered himself into the water. It was clear, running briskly among rocks, and Opio lay on the shallow bed with all of him under water but his face. The water was cold from the hills and soothing to his hot, tired flesh. Presently he sat up, took a handful of sand and began scrubbing himself clean.

While he was doing this he heard the hateful mimicking voice of one of the Oluoch brothers calling shrilly from the cave.

"Adhiambo! Adhiambo, fetch the water."

He saw Adhiambo get up from the fire he was building, take the waterpot and come down to the stream. He reached it somewhat below Opio, who was partly hidden under the bank. As he came near, Opio heard him muttering to himself. Then he stood hunched, deep in thought, and Opio knew that he believed himself to be alone.

Adhiambo waited there, his mouth working. He looked down at the pot he carried and suddenly straightened his great back.

"Draw water yourself," he said, "I'll do it no longer," and with sudden violence he smashed the pot to the ground and stood brooding. Then he sat in the litter of broken shards and began to weep.

Presently Oketch came out of the cave, either to see why Adhiambo was so long with the water or because he had heard the pot breaking and came for an explanation of the sound. He looked about, discovered Adhiambo sitting beside the stream and walked across the meadow to him. There he stopped and looked down curiously at the shaking shoulders.

"Adhiambo the Coward," he said, "are you deaf? Didn't you hear us call for water?"

Adhiambo said nothing in reply and Oketch kicked him.

Then Adhiambo rose up and seized Oketch by the throat and shook him like a sheaf of thatching grass. They were both big men, but at this moment Oketch was like a baby in Adhiambo's grip and he was picked up and flung onto the rocks of the stream, where he lay still, half in the water, and Opio knew that he was dead.

Adhiambo took two paces toward the cave, checked and came back and took the simi that Oketch wore slung round him, and Opio saw his mad and bloodshot eyes.

Then he strode up to the cave carrying the simi and, reaching the entrance, stopped and lurked.

Presently Ogalo and Omondi came out and Adhiambo sprang silently and killed them.

After that the rest came out bewildered and in ones and twos, few of them thinking to bring arms, and battle raged round the cave entrance. In the end they all lay there except Adhiambo and he stood bent and gasping, running with blood but still carrying his simi.

Not quite all. For while Opio watched, Adhiambo counted the dead and the purpose in his movements chilled Opio's heart. When it was done he began to scream in a cracked voice: "Kasuku! Kasuku, the son of Oluoch! You aren't here. Come out and then I'll have done with your family."

"This is surely madness," said Opio to himself, "but a cold madness," and he got out of the water and huddled on his kilt and waited to see what would happen.

Presently Kasuku dodged out of the cave past the waiting Adhiambo and ran along beneath the cliff face, scuttling from rock to rock like a startled hyrax.

"That one, at least, will never call Adhiambo coward again," said Opio.

Adhiambo gathered his strength and flung after the running Kasuku and it was wonderful that a man as sorely wounded as he obviously was could move so fast.

The two vanished in the scrub that grew close to the cliff face and Opio was alone and wondering what he should do. Presently he heard a clatter behind him and he turned to find Adhiambo. The man had lost the simi but now carried Kasuku's spear. Evidently he had come up in the shelter of the riverside trees, for Opio had heard or seen nothing. He was wheezing with pain and exhaustion and he swayed on his feet and looked at Opio.

Opio's spear was on the bank a dozen paces away. Adhiambo could do to him whatever his madness told him to.

"I think I must kill you, Opio," said Adhiambo.

"If you must, then you must," said Opio steadily, "though I see no reason for it."

"I see no reason either," replied Adhiambo, "but let's see if there could be one. Will you tell me my name, Opio?"

"You're Odhiambo," said Opio. "Odhiambo, the son of Imboya."

"Say it louder, Opio. Louder. Because my head is full of noises and it's difficult to be sure whether what is said is by you or by the other voices I hear."

Opio told him his name again and when he had done so Odhiambo remarked: "I thought you said that. I've not been named in that way for a long time. Too long. I'd become confused with another man."

"Put that spear down now, Odhiambo," said Opio softly. "You're badly hurt and your wounds should be seen to."

"I think I'll keep the spear," said Odhiambo after a moment's consideration. "Yes, I certainly think I'll keep it. Without the spear the other name might come back.

Perhaps it would be best if you went away now, Opio. A long way. Because I find that I've no wish to kill you and I'm afraid that my voices might tell me to do that and I think that if they do they should be obeyed. Things have got better since I did as they told me and I've no desire for them to be as they were again."

Then Opio left him and went up the bank a little with a naked cold place on the small of his back when he turned it on Odhiambo. But he reached the trees safely and stopped there and watched him from where he could not be seen himself.

Odhiambo muttered and swayed and then he turned and stumbled into the stream and out at the other side and across the plain without looking back. Presently Opio followed him, keeping at a distance.

He was easy to follow, for he went slowly, stopping often to rest, leaving a great trail of blood behind him in the dust and never looking back. Once he fell and Opio began to run forward, but stopped when Odhiambo got to his feet again and reeled on.

The sun began to go down and a wind swept across the plain from the direction of the lake and the dry branches of the thorns rattled together. Still Opio followed.

Then at last Odhiambo fell and stayed down. Opio went cautiously on and when he reached him the man had his back propped against a tree. He still held the spear and his eyes were closed, but he opened them when Opio came close.

They looked at each other silently.

Then Odhiambo said: "Tell me, Opio, and remember

it's bad to lie to a dying man, tell me truthfully. Do you think that I'm a coward?"

"No," replied Opio. "You're not a coward."

"I'm glad about that," said Odhiambo. "I'd begun to doubt."

Then he let go of the spear and sighed once and died.

3

Opio got the cattle home, some of them.

He went back to the cave and they were still chewing contentedly beside the stream. Then a thought came to him and he went in search of Kasuku. It was easy at first to follow Odhiambo's blood trail, but it was almost dark now, and soon quite so. Opio gave it up and returned to the cattle. He had no urge to go near the cave, so he built a fire and slept near the cattle, hoping they would rouse him if there was any alarm.

In the morning he searched again for Kasuku, either him or his body, but there was nothing to be found and Opio thought that he must have thrown away his spear the better to run, and so escaped Odhiambo's vengeance.

The place was very near to the edge of Kano, but the plain is broad and the river lies nearer to the Nandi side than it does to the Kisii and it took Opio three days to get home. The cattle were slow and the grass thin, so that he had to graze them half each day. At night it was more than one man could do to build a thorn boma that would be of any use, so they all had to take their chance. On the second night lions got among them and killed two. The rest scattered in the darkness, bellowing, and Opio took to a tree, leaving even his spear below, and spent a sleepless night there.

When dawn came and he saw the savage thorns he had climbed over without caring—indeed, without knowing they were there—and across whose teeth he had great difficulty in getting down, he grinned ruefully.

"Surely," he said to himself, "a coward's a strange kind of animal. I never felt the thorns last night any more than Odhiambo felt his wounds."

He spent half that day searching for the cattle, came first across two more bodies, half eaten, and then seventeen still alive, huddled together in thick bush. The rest he never saw again. He collected what was left to him and took them home safely.

Kasuku arrived two days after him. He was silent about what had happened, but he never contradicted the story Opio told. Indeed, he avoided him from that day on and lived quietly on his land, never going raiding again. Those who knew him said that his nature had changed and that he no longer grinned so readily.

Magere was back from his wars. The raid had not been a success and they had taken but few cattle. The Kisii had been awake and had moved back to the highlands.

He listened to Opio's story with interest.

"What a fool," he said in comment when it was finished.

"I don't think that Odhiambo was wholly to be blamed," protested Opio.

"I'm not speaking of him," said Magere. "He was far from being a fool. He did what he had to do and died. In the circumstances it was the best he could have done."

"The Boar?" Opio nodded. "Yes, perhaps he was a fool. But it was hard to see that Odhiambo would turn out like that, both when he was a coward and when he wasn't. I saw nothing that would have told me that it would come to what it did."

"Wrong again," said Magere. "The Boar wasn't a fool because he was what he was and couldn't help or change himself. Fools know better than they act. He didn't. That's why I wouldn't take him as a man of mine. He couldn't be taught."

"Then who's the fool?" asked Opio.

"You," said Magere, "for ever going on the raid."

4

One year after the rains had come and gone, just at the time when the little twisted cork trees flamed, all flowers as red as lobster claws, and no leaf, a young man called Oronde was brought to Onyango's household. He came from Sakwa.

Now where he lived was good country for everything but cattle. They could not live there because of a small brown hairy fly which bit them very viciously, and men too, like a red-hot spear tip. And after they had been bitten the cattle often sickened and died. Therefore the lakeside people of Sakwa lived in one place for gardens and the hunting and fishing, but their cattle they grazed inland where the country was higher. There they thrived, but much of the young men's time was spent away from home, guarding their family's herds.

It was a pleasant life, Oronde told them, among the smooth round hills with the little rivers brawling in the valleys below. The grazing grounds were owned by clans, the right being theirs by firm tradition, and trespassing on another clan's grass quickly led to fights among the herdsmen. But the rare quiet pools below, where the cattle were driven in the evening to drink, these were held in common, and sometimes a thousand beasts and fifty men met there at a time, and the young men joked and bathed and played sly tricks on each other. Such as swimming under water and pretending to be a crocodile grabbing an unsuspecting bather.

Also shared were great bomas with walls made of stones piled on each other. These were very old and indeed the Sakwa people do not know who made them because they themselves would never have thought of making a boma wall of stone. But they used them to impound the cattle at night and kept them repaired and were grateful. Because without these gifts from the past they would have been hard pressed to know what to do, for in the hills there were few trees for boma-making and especially the thorn tree is scarce and stunted.

This was the kind of life Oronde lived most of the year, following the cattle and hunting guinea fowl with arrows and taking his watch beneath the stars at night with his back against the stone slabs of the walls, still warm from the day's sun.

Now one day three cattle had been stolen by Dorobo and when the theft was discovered Oronde and two of his father's herdsmen had started after the thieves. They had tracked them as far as the Nandi Hills and had caught them up. The cows were recovered, but in the fight Oronde had been speared in the leg. The wound was deep and painful and it was impossible for him to walk. The herdsmen had carried him to the nearest Joluo clan and so he had come to Opio's family. After they had seen him in good hands they had set off back with the cattle and Oronde stayed until his wound was healed enough for him to walk.

He shared Opio's house and Opio grew fond of him.

Someone else grew fond of him also and that was Opio's youngest sister. She was called Andito and was the last of the Onyango girls to remain at home, for the elder had married away in Gem. She was a pretty girl and it was thought by many that she would make a fine housewife. She seemed anxious to demonstrate this to Oronde. Her cooking fire burned merrily half the day, and to

Oronde, lying on a good skin inside Opio's hut, came the finest porridge made from new millet, every grain soft and black and separate, thick milk from Andito's five goats and fish caught that very morning in the river. Opio noticed a notable improvement in his dinners (for he shared Oronde's meals), but he made no comment because he believed that when things were good they should not be fussed with or inquired after. As for Oronde, after his years on the hillsides of Sakwa—which though, no doubt, a fine life, must also have been somewhat hard in the lying—he found himself so drowned in comfort that he grew fat and showed little impatience to move on. He stayed to recover from his wound (and the herbs and simples Andito provided would have revived a corpse) and then he stayed to give a hand with the breaking of a new field for Andito, in return for all their kindness to him, and then . . . and then, he just stayed.

He was a fine young man, pleasant and courteous and quick to laugh and full to the brim of interesting tales which he told with great skill. Opio himself had no small reputation in this way and was delighted to meet a fellow artist. The two of them would sit by the hour capping each other's stories and the neighbors would come for miles to listen to them both, rocking with laughter which they tried to keep silent in case they lost a word, or shuddering with delightful horror at some tale of witchcraft. When this kind of story was being told, and the audience had lost touch with time, they would come to earth to find that it was late and perhaps dark. Then they would discover in themselves a most notable reluctance to walk home, and what with one thing and another Opio's father found himself standing nightly host to half the neighborhood and the outlay in porridge and chickens and goats greater than he liked.

However, at last, when his wound had been healed a month, Oronde found that there was nothing keeping him except that he wanted to stay, which, to a young man with a sense of what was right, seemed no good reason to continue eating his friends out of house and home. So he thanked them all and left for Sakwa. But before he went it was understood that when he had spoken to his family, and the bride-price had been paid, then Andito would become his wife.

Which was satisfactory for everyone, for the whole family liked him and it was time that Andito got married. Who better for her than Oronde as a husband? they asked, and meant it.

Time passed and almost a year later in the middle of the idle season two young men arrived from Sakwa waving freshly cut branches with the leaves still on them and driving five fat cows. They had come to fetch Oronde's bride to Sakwa and the cattle were proof that the offer was in earnest.

Then a bustle began.

Fine skins were prepared and decorated with beads. These were for the bride and the girls who would go with her to the wedding. Then when all the sewing was done and the two young men, friends of Oronde, had been feasted, at last, when all was ready, and Andito and the girls had stopped running back for things which they had forgotten, *then* a great party began the journey from Onyango's household. The bride went first, surrounded by chattering girls who would let no one else have anything to do with her. They were the friends of her youth, all of them unmarried, and they would see her safely to her husband's care, all the way to Sakwa. It was not improbable that they might find husbands for themselves there also, for one wedding often led to several others. Onyango followed, and his wife Anyango, and Opio and Magere and ten young warriors who were relatives of the family.

They went down through Kano, being given hospitality by the No clan (for all right-thinking men love a wedding party and do their best to smooth its way), then west along the lake shore, the warriors carrying bunches of grass tied to their spear blades to show they came in peace, but indeed they were welcomed and feasted everywhere, and slept every night under a roof. At last, guided by the two young men from Sakwa, they came to Oronde's clan lands, and Oronde and his father and all their people came out to meet them.

Oronde's clan were called the Owiti and his household was the greatest among them. They lived beside the true lake, which Opio had never seen before, only the gulf which ran into Kano. Here the water stretched south to the horizon, broken only by islands, and great waves fell on the shore, especially at evening when a wind got up blowing lakeward, often dropping only at morning. The Owiti clan were numerous and powerful, fishermen and herdsmen. They lived in villages, the huts nearer to each other than Opio was accustomed to, and the gardens were close to the water's edge because it was dry country and water had often to be carried from the lake if crops were to be grown during the dry season. The boats lay pulled up among the gardens, heavy canoes, each made from a single tree trunk, with grinning mouths painted on their bows, and eyes also, one each side, in red and white. It was said that the canoe spirits used these to get safely home on the darkest nights after the fishing was done.

The feasting lasted for days, as is the way at weddings when things are done in style. Lasted until old Onyango grew bad-tempered with over-eating and longed for his stool beneath his own hut eaves and the pipe that went with it. The one he had brought with him had been dropped and broken, and although he was lent another by his hosts and given the choice of a dozen, he mourned over small disasters as an old man does, and knew that only his own things in his own place would satisfy him.

At last Andito was firmly married to her Oronde (and happier than most they were to be with each other all their lives) and the time came for her family to leave her. But when this happened Opio stayed behind as a guest of his brother-in-law while the rest went back to Kano.

5

It was the time just before the long rains when the ground was too hard to cultivate and the winds too violent to fish and the sun too hot to hunt with pleasure. A waiting time when men were idle and edgy and searching for something to occupy themselves until the serious business of life claimed them again. And so at night they danced and when they were weary of this they told each other tales. Oronde was much in demand with the young men on these nights because, as has been said, he was a fine storyteller.

Now one night when he had finished a tale that had woven in and out and held every man there scarcely breathing in case they lost a twist in its course, one had sighed at the end and said that he had never heard a better tale, nor one better told.

Opio, who had also listened, said that it was indeed a tale worth hearing and that their clan had a rare artist in Oronde, but that if he had been telling it he would have dealt with certain events this way and that. And he went on to argue the changes he would have made in a way that he often did privately with Oronde, for they took their gifts seriously and enjoyed discussing the craft of words. It was one of the bonds between them.

The young man, however, took this to be a slight upon the story they had heard and upon the teller and the clan he came from, and he said, with some heat, "I suppose they have better stories told in Kano."

"They do indeed tell stories there and some of them aren't difficult to listen to," replied Opio.

"And I suppose you tell them," said the young man.

Opio paused at this, because he had no wish to quarrel with his hosts. But still he had his dignity to defend and it was not the habit of his people to deny a skill which was known to be possessed.

"I can tell a story among others," he said firmly.

"I'd bet a heifer Oronde would put you down in story-telling!" cried the young man, and others hurried to add to the wager.

Opio looked at Oronde doubtfully, because he was a guest and had to behave with discretion.

Oronde grinned and said, "It would be interesting, Opio, to see what the result would be between you and me."

Then Opio felt satisfied that no harm would come of it, whatever the outcome, and the challenge was made. There were customs which ruled how a matter of this kind should go, and so at once an elder was sought out. When it was explained to him he declared the way it should be done. A day was given to both to prepare and then at evening they would draw lots and the winner would choose whether to tell that night or the next. Also, since it was not possible to judge between a light-hearted story of foolishness and pride and another of fear or heroism, between a story of animals or one of men, a theme had to be set which both must hold to or lose.

That was how he said it must be done.

"And what shall be the theme of the tales?" they cried.

"Mm," said the elder, and rubbed his nose thoughtfully. "Now give a man time to think and room to do it in."

They waited expectantly.

"Ah, yes," he said at last. "Both stories must deal with witches and witchcraft. That's always a subject of some interest. Witches and witchcraft shall be the theme."

And so it was decided.

The next evening almost the whole clan assembled on the shore, beneath the gnarled and ancient sausage trees that grew there, in order to hear the first tale. They perched on stranded boats or lay in the soft sand. It was a fine night for the business in hand, a moon but no wind and the waves small and almost soundless. The people waited impatiently to learn who should tell first.

The elder decided this quite simply by putting two beans of the cork tree into a gourd which had a neck just wide enough to receive a hand and arm. One bean had the usual crimson spot upon its glossy black skin, the other, as happens with one in a hundred, was unmarked. He shook the gourd and offered it first to Opio and then Oronde, and they each groped for and drew out a bean. Opio's bean was unmarked, and so, by custom, the choice was his.

"Let Oronde tell first," he said, and the contest began.

Oronde sat on a stool and pretended to consider what he should say. Then he raised his head and said to the people, "It is in my mind to tell a tale."

"Tell it," they replied in one voice.

"Perhaps some here have heard," he went on, "a certain

noise upon their thatch. It comes at night, from outside. It is like rats but not *quite* like rats. It could be a house snake but isn't. It sounds like feet upon the roof, but the feet have claws. Are there any here who've heard this?"

"We've heard it," they said.

"I'll explain that noise," said Oronde, "and when the story is finished anyone can believe it who wants to."

Everyone settled his hams more firmly and prepared to believe.

THE WITCH OF ALEGO

Many years ago there lived in Alego a woman whose name was Chinyunja. She was called this for the very good reason that her husband's name was Nyunja.

She was a lean and energetic woman, always busy, always hungry, always angry, always up in the morning at cockcrow, rattling the porridge stick in the pot; with a voice that went through your head like the howl of a child with the colic.

"Nyunja!" she would scream. "Nyunja! Get up and clear the rocks from the top field. The rains will be here in a minute and we must sow and get a little more grain than last year."

"Nyunja! Get up and take the white goat to Yala Market. It looks sick and might die. They won't know us that far away and we could get a few chickens for it."

Poor Nyunja. He was fat and easygoing when he married, but he didn't stay that way for long. No more sitting in the shade with a few friends discussing the reason for this and the other. Now he moiled and toiled from dawn till dusk and his voice grew thin and anxious and when he laid down his hoe to breathe a bit he glanced over his shoulder expecting to hear his wife screech.

For she wanted to rise in the world. Rich she determined they should be and rich they became. She scraped and saved and worked and schemed and drove Nyunja to do the same until his hair grew thin on top. Eh! How they worked! A field cleared here and a beast bought there and so things grew. The flock of goats increased from six to sixteen and then to sixty, until their neighbors who, when they had noticed them at all, had only done so to smile in a superior way, began to take a little more interest.

Now Chinyunja and Nyunja had but one child, a son who was called Omolo. He grew up to be a great hulking slab of a lad with a face as round and smooth and placid as the bottom of a well. Perhaps not so bright in the head as some, but a good boy, who never complained when his mother gave him the best cut off the joint or told him to rest in case he overtaxed his strength.

For it must be said, Chinyunja made a fool of herself over Omolo. How she doted! Nothing was too good for Omolo.

"Eh! Look at the size and *presence* of him! How handsomely he yawns and gracefully he stretches. Such dignity! Such weight! If the world gives him his deserts what a chieftain he'll make! And if I've my way and his father does his duty he *shall* get his deserts. He must be found a wife. Not a common chit, oh, no, only a girl from the best of families will do for my Omolo. It's time we set to work on this. We're rich enough. There must be a feast, a grand feast with no expense spared and all the really *substantial* people invited. They'll come and see the flock and the fine fields and the elegance and plenty of everything. Eh! That'll bring their daughters trotting, anxious to be married into such a family as we are."

That was what Chinyunja decided and told her husband her plans, and although he sighed and longed for a quiet life he was quite sure there was no chance of getting one, so he did as he was told and set about his share of the preparations.

When the harvest was in Chinyunja made ready for the feast. What a turmoil there was!

First, of course the beer had to be brewed, for whoever heard of a feast without beer? Beer in floods. The two silent little servant girls (daughters of poor relations, got cheap) hurried to and fro from the river with pots of water on their heads, and millet came from the store and was spread on reed mats beside the kitchen shelter so that every trace of husk or stem might be removed. They looked like deep gold-colored carpets spread in the sun. The great black pots stood shoulder to shoulder on the fire and the low murmur of their bubbling was to be heard the day long.

Nyunja and a neighbor cut leafy boughs and built a shelter where all the guests could sit, since they would be too many for the house to hold and all far too important for the sun to fall on their heads while they ate and drank.

Even Omolo was stirred up and sent to make a round

of the farms with instructions to say at each: "Our family has brewed beer and would be grateful if you would honor us by giving an opinion as to its taste and strength. It will be ready the day after tomorrow."

This was the form invitations took in Alego and Chinyunja had made him say it after her a couple of hundred times until he had it by heart, and succeeded so well that for years afterward, if he was woken a little suddenly, he was likely to blink twice and begin, "Our family has brewed beer and would be grateful—" before he was told sharply to rouse himself and shut up.

The great day came and all stood ready. Heaps of ripe fruit and mounds of cooked vegetables, calabashes of honey and pyramids of boiled eggs heaped on broad banana leaves. All mustered for those who like such things, but trifles fit for children. More for the look of the thing than for use. More serious was the fine fat goat, its joints hanging in the shade, ready for the roast, and most, the great pots of beer, cool, still and important, like elders at a feast waiting for the good word "Begin!"

As the morning grew hot the guests arrived, dignified old men who clasped the hands of the Nyunja family, murmured their greetings and then sat in the bower made for their comfort. They settled their stools firmly, fanned themselves with fly whisks made from white cows' tails, opened snuff gourds and gravely offered their neighbors a pinch. When Nyunja and Omolo hurried in with the first of the pots they put the snuff aside, selected long reeds from a pile at hand, dipped them into the beer and sucked.

Nyunja and Omolo anxiously watched that first long

silent draw, which was a question. And the second, which was a judgment. Then the old men sighed, their fly whisks fell still, their wrinkled eyelids closed with pleasure. This was a beer worthy of their honor and importance.

The Nyunja family sighed also, with relief. If things went on as they were beginning then all was as good as made.

As with all good feasts there was plenty of time. No hurry, no hurry at all. After an hour the first pots were empty and reinforcements hurried forward. The old men dipped their straws again, but with a certain air of anxiety. Would these pots hold a brew as excellent as the first? There *were* households (it would be kinder not to name them) where the second round showed a sad falling off. Ah, no. This was as fine as they had already tasted.

A gentle babble of praise went up like smoke. Praise for the beer, the brewer, the hospitality. Nyunja wrung his hands with pleasure, and his wife, who was outside with her ear against the wall of the bower, hugged herself and danced a few stiff steps for joy.

It was true that one skinny but important old man (he owned at least a hundred cows) was heard to doubt that the supply would last until night, but no one took any notice of him, since he was known always to be gloomy.

Time passed. The guests drank and gossiped and purred like cats before the fire. First one and then another asked for meat.

"At once. It'll come," said Nyunja eagerly, and signed to his son, who ran to tell his mother.

The skinny old man (he employed quite twenty servants) piped to his neighbor: "I wish our host knew that I haven't a tooth in my head. Then he might have cooked for me the liver and tongue."

Nyunja heard, as he was meant to do, and ran with instructions to his wife.

"Be quiet," she answered. "And get out of my way. When have I not known what I'm about? I wish the same could be said for you. Off with you back to the guests and leave this to me."

So Nyunja went back and Chinyunja bared her arms and began to cook.

The fire was just right. It had started life enormous, but now had shrunk to a glowing mass of embers. The stones round it were red-hot and the air quivered above them. She took the joints of goat and larded them and spitted them and hung and basted them, and crooned with pleasure as she did so. It was a hot day and the fire was fierce. It promised to be thirsty work, but beside her was a pot of her finest beer and as she cooked she sipped.

No hurry. It must be done well. It must be cooked as never meat was cooked before.

She waited, sipping steadily as she watched the joints, and every now and then she basted and the fat ran hissing into the fire.

She squatted on her heels and drank, and as she drank she tasted the meat.

Not nearly ready yet.

"Ah, how good it is to be the finest cook in Alego and . . . Alego? No! The finest cook in all Luo . . . and to entertain great company . . . really this meat is delicious . . . and to drink the rich beer I've brewed so skillfully . . . another cupful would do no harm . . . but is the meat done yet? Mm? Not yet. Better try a morsel from that leg, though. It hangs nearer the fire than the rest. Never, never have I tasted finer . . . a little more of this . . . and a little more of that. . . ."

Chinyunja was not used to beer (all those years of skimping) and what with this, and the heat of the day, and the fire and the success of her plans, she was not at all herself.

When at last Nyunja and Omolo came to fetch the meat it was gone. Chinyunja had eaten everything.

A WHOLE GOAT!

At last the hungry guests came trooping from the shelter to see what delayed the roast. They saw. Then they lifted their proud old faces from the unbecoming sight, drew their cloaks tightly round them against the cold night air, and went home.

The skinny old man went last (he owned a dozen fields and had ten daughters).

"Thank you for the meat, Nyunja and Omolo," he squeaked. "It was de-licious."

He knew how a properly conducted household should treat a guest.

When they had gone Nyunja straightened himself up, raised his fists to the darkening sky and cursed his wife.

And Chinyunja?

She behaved most strangely. She seemed to shrink. She shrieked and tore her clothes. She ran in circles, each wider than the last, faster and faster, until, with a dreadful screech, she flew into the air, her dress flapping behind her, circled once like a great black bat and vanished into the night.

"So now, friends," said Oronde, "when the wind from the lake howls across swamp and hill and men bar the door and children rest quietly beside their mothers, and those feet come clawing at the thatch; *then* you may say to your troubled children when they ask: 'That? That's Chinyunja. Come to beg us to return to her feast.'

"But perhaps," added Oronde, "perhaps it's all nonsense."

6

The day after Oronde's telling he and Opio walked along the shore to a Samia market.

The borders of Samia lay close to the Owiti, if border it could be called, because here, where settlement had lasted longer, the tribes were often mixed up. It was only on the frontiers of the Joluo movement, among the Kano and Kisumu clans, that there was a firm line drawn round territory and men lived on their toes, suspicious of their neighbors.

The Samia were the old people of the lake's northern

coast, a sturdy, quick-witted folk, fishermen, hunters and traders. Their land was a tangle of marshes, inshore islands and broad pans of stagnant water. Here two great rivers came to the lake and in this low-lying country they divided again and again. It was rich and fertile enough where it was not sodden with water, but difficult to move in unless one had been born to it. The Joluo despised the Samia a little (they were indeed somewhat contemptuous and sorry for all people who were not Joluo) and had in the past accused them of not being entirely human, differing, for one thing, by having webbed feet. But this accusation was made after several disastrous campaigns in the mud. The Samia were quite content to be despised so long as they kept their land, and this they had done, so far, most successfully, because of its nature, their own sturdiness, and also because of a habit they had of poisoning arrows.

Their far border was with Uganda and the tribes near it were small and poor and of little importance. But Samia canoes went far along the Uganda coast, as far as the Old Kingdoms, and also to the most distant islands of the open lake. These were beyond sight of the furthest fishing grounds and almost legendary to other people who hated to lose sight of land, but not to the Samia, who handled boats with a daring and skill no other tribe possessed. Because of this voyaging the markets of Samia were rich in many things unknown elsewhere and all the peoples living near used them. And also they kept a peace, both coming and going, for it seemed to all sensible that something useful should not be ruined by a moment's foolishness.

The greatest of these markets was at a place called Mundere, only a few miles from the Oronde household. There was always some buying and selling here, but every now and then word went round of what was called a Great Market. Then people flocked in hundreds. They brought with them the choicest of all they grew or made and with it bargained for upward of a week for luxuries. There was only one other way for a man to buy what caught his eye, and that was to offer cowrie shells, for these were the common coin of Africa, accepted everywhere. The cowrie came from the salt waters of the Indian Ocean. No man of these inland tribes had ever been there, the sea being as distant and unreal a place as the Great White-Topped Mountain of story where the gods lived, or that country beneath the earth where a great snake waited for the ghosts of the dead, and shook the world whenever he woke from sleep. But from the sea the cowries came, slipping from hand to hand, exchanged, bequeathed, stolen; filtering inland until every man of substance had a bag of them buried in the floor of his hut, and every pretty girl a few to sew on her marriage skin.

It was a Great Market now and Oronde wished to show Opio one of the sights of his country, and Opio to taste a new experience as a storyteller of repute should do, for if his mind is not fed with new things the skill grows thin and dies.

The market was set in a grove of trees beside the lake, some of them so close to the water that their roots writhed into it. A thriving, babbling place, stretching for half a mile, where men, and even more often women, drove bargains with all their hearts and strength. They sneered and even wept, pleaded and grew angry, exploded with scornful laughter and turned away indignantly (returning rapidly if the price budged), and all to add one handful to a basket of grain. It was a contest rather than a purchase. The hope of more kept them happy and the exercise healthy. If it took a week, well, Africa had plenty of time.

Opio and Oronde walked between shining heaps of millet and corn, cowpeas and sunflower seeds, peppers, okra, beans and berries, poured out from leather sacks and patterned baskets onto mats laid on the ground. Mangoes and pumpkins, avocados and guavas, stood in mounds. There were whole stalks of bananas, yellow, purple, black and green, a single one of them a man's load, and huge warty jack fruit, split and oozing with sticky ripeness and clotted with flies.

In the shade between those selling were the troops of donkeys which had brought the produce and every so often their braying added a weird note to all the noises and everyone paused to listen and laugh. Donkeys were newly come to these parts from the north and many men saw them for the first time at Mundere Market.

The two wandered on, pausing at ranks of soapstone pots and pipe bowls from the Kisii Hills, reed matting from Kavirondo, ironwood clubs and sticks from Teso. Hides stank to heaven beside beaded leather caps and tanned cloaks sewn all over with cowries and seeds and red, white and black beads. These came from the cattle tribes, and, sitting near them, somewhat apart and silent, a group of Nyangori smiths offered iron cowbells, two tongues of metal bent over and married, the clappers heavy iron rings swung on thongs. Small, wiry, morose men these, their hands and arms covered with old burns that looked like shining snail-trails on the black flesh. Opio admired their spears and simis, awls, knives and branding irons, smelted with charcoal from the rain forest and cold-hammered in secret, for the smith's work reeked of witchcraft, and was not to be watched by the uninitiated.

And then they came upon a group of tall men, red-skinned, with still, narrow faces. They stood before three long canoes drawn up on the beach. There were several women with them busy over cooking fires, some of them very beautiful. They were of another race than any known to Opio.

"Who are these?" he asked Oronde.

"Wafango. They come from the islands the Samia call Umfango. But the name they are usually given is the Snake People. Come and see what they are selling."

Standing somewhat apart from the group was a girl, and before her on the ground was what at this distance seemed to be a vast mat of intricate dazzling pattern. When they were near, Opio saw that it was hundreds of snakeskins all skillfully cured so that the undersides were as mealy-white and soft as fine ground flour. He remarked those of the great green pythons of the rivers, the more vivid green of the slender tree mamba, the yellow diamonds of slow and dangerous puff adders, the blacks and reds of spitting cobras. But there were many skins there from snakes which he had never seen and to which he could give no name. Like all his people he hated and feared snakes and he wondered at the cold courage and cunning of men who could kill them in such quantities, or bear to handle their cold heavy bodies afterward.

Then he looked up from the skins and became aware of the girl standing beyond, and she smiled at him and he thought her to be more beautiful than any woman he had ever seen.

To his surprise she spoke the Dholuo, with a kind of sing-intonation and many words that were strange to him. But her speech was easily understandable.

When he asked her about this she smiled and said: "But of course. We who live in the islands travel far to trade. We must speak with all men. Also our people came from the kingdoms of Uganda, as yours did long ago. Our tongues are two fingers of the same hand."

They talked quietly together and presently she asked him if he saw anything he wished to buy.

"Not snakeskin," said Opio. "Only our witch doctors wear them and I have no skill in that direction. But the crocodile hide there would look handsome round the edge of a shield. I must return another time to consider it, for now I have nothing to buy with. Will you be at the market tomorrow?"

She told him that her uncle and the others from the islands would stay as long as the market lasted, even longer, for they had other business with the Samia. Perhaps in all a month.

So Opio left her and he and Oronde went back to Sakwa. But the girl's face hung in his mind and he was pleased that he had left trailing an excuse to meet her again.

7

That evening Opio stood up and looked at the Owiti clan assembled before him. He said, "It's in my mind to tell a tale."

"Tell it," answered the people.

"Listen then," replied Opio. "You must know that inland from here, where the hills are rumpled like a skin tumbled from a bed and the clouds lie late in the morning, there live a people called the Bunyore. They are not a numerous people, there are only a few thousand of them, and they perch their houses on hills out of the damp and the way of strangers, make their gardens below and take life as it comes. Their favorite word is *tomorrow*. 'We'll do it *tomorrow*, God willing.'

"But, as you also know, there is one thing for which they are famous, and that is rain-making.

"They say that they can make the rain come when they've a mind to, and all of you know it's true. And so, far and wide, down in the flat country where rain is scarce, or in distant Kisii and the Nandi Hills, even far away on the borders of Uganda, when the dust blows through the trees and the leaves shrivel, and the cattle grow thin and hang their heads and the rain doesn't come and doesn't come; *then* the people say, 'We must send for the Bunyore.'

"And they do. With a rich present to hurry the business up.

"Presently, in his own time, there comes a ragged old man with a sly eye and a bag full of mysteries. A Bunyore rain-maker. You've seen him.

"He listens politely to the tale of misfortune, the rain that promised at nightfall and went away by day, the beans that were sown in hopes and eaten by mice and the stream run dry. Politely, calmly and with a hint of weariness. He has heard it all before.

"What does he do? For a week he pokes about muttering charms and spells, or maybe he is only grumbling under his breath at the quality of the meals provided. Who knows? He keeps an eye on the way the hills look in the early dawn and he taps the hard ant heaps with a stick and listens to the answering note of the creatures below. He watches the birds come to roost at night, especially the sunbird. Then one day he sits down near a lonely tree or rock and begins to take out an odd-looking bone or two and a queerly shaped bottle. It is *then* that he notices for the first time the people crowding close with their mouths open and he coughs and gives them a hard stare. Then they go away hastily.

"So no one knows exactly what he does, but the next day he's gone with his bag over his shoulder, back to Bunyore, and in a day or a week the rain begins.

"The most famous family of rain-makers in Bunyore are called the Vagimba and the most skilled of all the Vagimba was a man called Mugimba who lived a vast time ago and started the trade.

"Now isn't all I've said true?"

"It's true," said the people.

"Then listen," said Opio, "and I'll explain how it all began."

He paused for a moment; the face of the girl he had seen that afternoon came to him and he smiled and felt such a power of words within him as he had never known before. Then he shut his heart to everything but his story and began.

MUGIMBA, THE RAIN-MAKER

Far from Bunyore in lakeside Ukwala, where today the land is as dry as a bone, there appeared long ago an old woman.

It was evening and the folk were ready to launch the boats when a storm blew up in the twinkling of an eye, and everyone ran for their houses out of the rain and wind, and left the boats glistening wet. The old woman came up the shore with driven leaves scampering past her and she might have come out of the lake for all anyone had ever seen of her before.

"Come in, Mother," they shouted from the doorways of the huts. "Come in, for this is no night to be out."

So into the hut where the fishermen were crowded she came and sank down with a sigh and a shake of her wet hair.

They looked at her.

What a sight! A tiny shriveled old dame, dressed in rags, with scraps of waterside weed dabbed all over and hands like claws. And older-looking than anyone had ever seen a woman before.

They gave her a bite to eat and asked: "Where do you come from, Mother? And what are you doing here?"

But she said nothing sensible, only cackled, "Heh, heh!" and mumbled her end of corncake.

Then they smiled secretly at each other and tapped their foreheads.

"Poor old body, her wits are gone."

But they didn't smile for long. For the storm went on and went on and no one had ever seen the like of it. The thunder roared and the lightning split the rocks and blasted the trees. The wind screamed across the lake and squalled through cracks in the walls and a man never knew whether his thatch was on his roof or scattered over half Africa until the rain poured into his bed. The snakes came out of their flooded holes and into the houses and food ran short and rats grew bold and fought with the children for the porridge. The lake rose day by day and the fishermen pulled their boats higher and higher until they lay between the huts. And still the water followed until it ate into the walls and house after house fell sideways with a sigh and a sucking noise of dissolving mud. Then families took their gear and lodged with luckier folk who had built on higher ground.

Still it rained and thundered and blew, day in, day out.

Then the people knew that the land was bewitched and where to lay the blame, and they went in a body to the old woman who had come from nowhere and still lived on their charity.

"Old crone," they roared, "you're a witch! Undo what you've done!"

But she only cackled.

Then they grasped their sticks and spears more tightly and shouted: "The weather came with you and perhaps it'll go with you. Up, you old hag, and out of the land, or we'll beat you to death!"

And so they might have done had not the old woman stood up and looked awesome. She pointed two hooked fingers at them and the thunder bellowed and lightning ran along her skinny arms and her eyes glittered like burning salt. "So," she hissed, "so I'm to go, am I? There's to be no bowl of food and a place by the fire for an old woman and a stranger. Is that the way it is? Very *well,* I'll go. Go where folks are kinder and don't blame their misfortunes on the weak. And since you say I brought the rain, then I'll take it with me, and I wish you luck without."

Then she went in a flutter of rags, running along the shore and into the murk of the storm, gone before a man could take so much as a step, and it was wonderful that a crone so old could be so nimble.

"Well, good riddance to her," they said doubtfully. "Perhaps we'll have some decent weather and be able to get a bit of fish."

And so they did. The rain rolled away and the sun shone and they rebuilt the houses that had fallen and the young people danced again in the still hot nights and forgot their troubles. Until three months later when the rain should have come for the corn planting. But it didn't. Not that year, or the next, or the next. There was no rain in

Ukwala, that is not to say *rain*. Only a few showers from the lake which did more harm than good. The people who lived by the water's edge made do on fish and carried water from the lake to tiny patches of garden; the rest crowded to the river or went away and the land grew empty and dry. Eh, how dry!

But what of the old woman?

She next appeared in Teriki, and a weary journey she must have had of it, for it's a long, sad way from Ukwala to Teriki. The forest begins there, or did in those days, the real rain forest of the hills, with trees that seem to soar up to the sky, all lanky legs and tiny heads. Your feet are silent on a carpet of leaves and the light slants between the trunks like sunlight through the rafters of a great unthatched hut, and you talk in whispers. The Terik live there, in the long narrow glades. They keep a few cows and hunt a little and grow their vegetables at the edges of the forests. They are a secretive people, greatly given to magic, and their neighbors keep their distance.

The old crone appeared at the house of a man called Arap Chemjor, a fat little man with a way of looking sideways at you when he spoke and an important strut when he walked. He had a reputation of sorts as a doctor and had been known to cure stomach-aches by casting knucklebones on a square of hide. But he asked a pretty sum for doing so.

"Eh!" said the crone as she sank down beside his door, "but I'm weary."

"Maybe you've traveled far?" said Arap Chemjor politely, as he looked his guest over with care.

"Far? Aye, too far," she replied. "I could do with a morsel to eat and a bed beside the fire."

"As it happens," said Chemjor, "I've very little in the house at the moment. As it happens. I'm only a poor doctor and spell-maker, in a local kind of way, you understand. And times are bad."

"I could pay you well for it," said the crone.

"Ah, that's different," said Chemjor. "With what, may I ask? You'll forgive the question but . . . well . . ." and he made a little jerk with his hands at her rags. "Perhaps you're an heiress in disguise?"

"I could teach you an art that would make your fortune," she said.

"Hm," said Chemjor. "Magic?"

"Magic," she replied. "Magic that will freeze the marrow in your bones and make your hair stand on end like the fur of a spitting cat. Magic and power that will fetch men to your door, bringing wealth and cattle. That is, if your nerves are strong enough to bear it."

"Come in," said Chemjor. "There's a nice piece of ox-hump I was keeping for tomorrow."

And so later, when the ox-hump was only a memory and the fire was burning low, they put their heads together and she began to teach him her magic.

"Now look," she said. "First you need the white bones of an ant bear's tail, clean-picked by crows and taken with the dew still on them," and she took these from beneath her rags and spread them on the floor with a twist of her wrist.

"Next, new oil from a python's fat," and she emptied a

green slow-pouring oil from a tightly stoppered gourd into a tiny bowl.

"Next, a sodom-apple, plucked where dead men's bones are buried," and the hard, green, bitter fruit dropped with a plop into the oil.

"All these are powerful and dangerous things," she said, and chuckled horribly.

Chemjor eyed them doubtfully and drew back a little, and far away in the forest he heard the first deep mutter of a storm.

"Perhaps it would be best if we began in a small way," he ventured, but the crone was deep in her mutterings and heard nothing.

"Next there are the words that must be said," she crooned, and she shut her eyes and rocked her body and said the words. Awful words, and the skin of Chemjor's head crept on his skull. Then the storm burst outside and lightning stabbed through chinks in the walls and Chemjor screamed in terror and cowered away.

"Then words and actions married be," she chanted, and her claws stretched up and the rain came down like a wall on Teriki, and, outside, the little animals that live in holes in the earth and crannies in the trees chattered with fear and scrabbled at the door for shelter.

"Stop!" yelled Chemjor. "For pity's sake, *stop*!"

Outside, the neighbors ran from their houses and stood dazed and battered in the storm.

"What's happening?" one cried, and another answered:

"Whatever it is, it's at Chemjor's house. Look!"

And when they looked they saw that the house was as

red as blood and the lightning licked up the walls like flames round a pot. Then they seized sticks and spears and bows and ran to question Chemjor, and when they got there he staggered out with his hands over his eyes and his hair standing up like the fur of a spitting cat.

"It's a witch!" he cried. "Save me, neighbors, from a witch!"

Then they chased her through the trees—she ran like an antelope—and the hunt went as far as the hill called Muuzatsi and there stopped in the mist that seemed to fall behind her as she fled and wept. The last they saw she was running hard, downhill, in the direction of Bunyore.

And now we come, at last, to Mugimba.

He lived in a little house on the side of a hill and he was poor and alone in the world, but he took things as they came and his favorite word was *tomorrow*. "It'll be better *tomorrow,* God willing."

There had been a storm the night before, over Teriki way, a big one by the look of it, and Mugimba had said to himself: "Ah, the rains are beginning. It's time to dig and plant."

So that is what he had done all the next day, and come home tired but cheerful, to find, sitting by the cold stones of his hearth, a tiny wrinkled old woman, very tired and sad.

"Good evening, Grannie," said Mugimba. "What are you doing here?"

She pointed a shaking finger at him and asked, "Are you like the rest?"

"I don't know who the rest are, Grannie," answered

Mugimba, "but my mother, when she lived, used to say that I was like no one else that she'd ever met. I've often wondered since what she meant."

"They're a poor, mean, miserable lot," grumbled his visitor.

"Maybe they've troubles," said Mugimba. "Folks with troubles get crotchety. But Grannie, it's late to discuss these things on an empty stomach. I'm tired and hungry and you look the same. Let's get a fire going on these stones and warm up a mouthful of porridge."

And so they warmed the porridge and ate it with a little honey poured on top, which is a good way when the honey is thick and dark as amber and tastes of the wild mint the bees have fed on.

When the last scrap was gone the old woman sat back on her hunkers, and her hands were no longer trembling, nor her eyes so wild. She looked at her host with approval.

"You're a proper young man," she said, "and kind. I've a mind to reward you for your goodness."

"Don't bother, Grannie," said Mugimba, wiping out the empty pot with a wisp of grass, "for I'm sure that you're very welcome."

"In the name of Gogo, stop fiddling with that pot and sit down and pay attention," she snapped. "Who would have thought it would be so difficult to give men what they wanted."

"All right, Grannie," said Mugimba, and he did as she wished. "Now what is it you have to tell me?"

She bent forward.

"Do you want to be rich, young man? Do you want to

have cattle as trees have leaves, servants to fetch and carry and power that brings respect and a ready ear to your slightest wish? Would you like these things, Mugimba?"

"That would be very nice, Grannie," he said. "A goat now. That would be useful for milk and there's good grazing in the valley bottom. I've often thought about having one."

"Bah, a goat! A goat, he says!"

"It's not to be sneezed at," said Mugimba.

"Listen, I can teach you how to bring the rain when you've a mind to. Men would pay you richly for a loan of that gift."

"Yes, indeed, Grannie, but we shan't need it this year, unless I'm mistaken. It's coming up nicely. There was a fine storm last night over Teriki way and I'm sure it'll be here in a day or so."

The old crone drew herself up in her rags and her eyes flashed and she looked mighty proud.

"And who made that storm, I ask you?" she said. "I did. D'you hear?"

"I'm sure you did, Grannie, but don't get excited, it's bad for you. Now what about getting some sleep. I should be up early tomorrow morning and—"

"Oh, thunderbolts and whirlpools!" she screamed in a passion. "Is there no way in this world of making what must be said plain?" And she smashed her fist on the bottom of the pot which lay upturned between them, so that it broke the clay and went right through. Mugimba thought it best to say nothing to this and so he watched her sit back and suck her knuckles and close her eyes and mumble to herself until she grew calmer. Then she began again, speaking very slowly and carefully.

"Listen," she said. "Just listen and if you wish me well don't speak, *and I will teach one fool of a man to better himself if it is the last thing I do*!"

And so she did.

Out came the bones and the oil and the hard green fruit, and the spells were said. When the storm began to mutter, Mugimba remarked, "That's good, it's closer than it was last night," and when the rain marched toward them like the rumble of a great rock coming down a hillside he observed, "I'm glad I got the garden dug today." When the storm burst with the noise of a falling mountain, and the lightning coiled about the room like a shoal of eels round bait, he said: "It's bad tonight. But better come hard now than later when the crops begin to grow."

But by the time the last spell was made and the old woman sank exhausted into her rags, and the storm calmed to a steady whisper of rain upon the thatch and you could hear the dry earth drinking outside; by then, Mugimba knew the secret, and his life's work was begun.

He built a little house for the old woman lower down the hill (it was nearer to go for her water) and there she lived and cared for the garden he dug for her. In time she grew milder in her manner and less frightening to ordinary folk, and proved a fine hand at the making of honey beer.

But the fame of Mugimba's new art spread far and soon he was called in by people from distant parts to bring the rain when they needed it, and a fine living he made and grew rich and fat. Indeed so fat that he found the journeys over the hills tiring and was content to teach the work to his sons when they came, and they, in their turn, to theirs, down to this day.

But neither he nor his ever tried their skill in Ukwala. They knew better. Whatever the old woman had done to the weather there had been done for good and all, and it's still dry.

Eh, how dry!

When Opio had finished his story there was a long silence.

Then a man released a breath that he did not know he had been holding, and others remembered to move and relieve cramped legs, and yet another said a long, wondering, "E-e-eh!"

Then Oronde said from his place beside Opio: "There's no need to go further into the matter. It was a good story and a better one than I could have told."

And when it came to the turn of the rest who had listened to speak, they agreed with him. Because although, in the ordinary way of life, a man must hold to his clan and give no other best, when it is a matter of the great crafts, song and dance and the telling of tales, one must be just and award the praise where it is due. And indeed it is not a question of this people or that, for the making of a great thing is beyond clan or people, and belongs to all men who have the wit to understand it.

8

The next day Opio went back to the market at Mundere and talked with the girl from the islands, and for a handful of cowries he bought the crocodile skin that was to garnish his shield.

Her name was Teri, and in the days that followed he went often to see her. They met at first in the market place and walked together on the shore, knowing that it was pleasant to be together, but then the feeling of these meetings changed without either of them being able to see the moment it happened, and then they slipped away secretly, not wishing anyone else to know they were together, hiding their happiness in each other in the trees beyond the market.

She told him of the far islands of the Great Lake where she and her people lived, and of how they had come there in the past. It seemed that all their great men were descended from younger sons of the Old Kings of Uganda, men who had fled from the kingdom each time a reigning king died and the eldest son searched for his brothers to kill them and make his own seat safe. Teri's father's father had come in this way with a fleet of canoes after a lost battle, and with the king's executioners breathing hot upon his neck. He had been followed to the islands by servants and friends who had gambled upon his winning the struggle for the royal stool. They lost with him and knew that there could only be one end for them if they stayed.

Teri had a gift and understanding for words which Opio recognized to be equal to his own and she made him see clearly the great houses of the islands and the proud men who lived in them, eaten with discontent and dreaming of returning to the Kingdoms. Even now canoes came and went from Uganda and men whispered and plotted, with the women and children out of earshot, before returning in the early dawn. To men like these the islands were a prison; they longed for the space and wealth of the mainland, lusted for power among a rich and powerful people. But Teri loved her home. She told him of all the small warm things of her life, of gardens full of melons growing golden in the litter of their dead leaves (for the islands grew melons beyond compare), of bright green birds with yellow beaks which when caught young would live in the houses and talk like men, of swimming in rough water, for all the island people swam as soon as they could walk, of the patterned bark-cloth the women made, fine and supple and soft as a web. In this talk of her home there was always a sense of light and sun, and behind all a glimpse of a great curve of water bending round everything.

Opio listened to her and watched her smile at her own memories and he knew that he loved her and would always do so.

When he told her of this she nodded sadly. She had recognized her own love for him since the day he had bought the skin.

"Then," said Opio, "I must go to your people and discuss the bride-price and you'll have to advise me over this because people's customs differ and I'd not like to look a fool."

She shook her head.

"There'll be no bride-price," she said, "because there'll not be any marriage between us. In the eyes of my people I'm a daughter of the ruling house of the Baganda and you're a tribesman of the Kavirondo coast. To them such a marriage would be impossible."

"My family has been heard of as well," said Opio angrily. "They own cattle and land and a certain place in men's estimation. Ask the great tribes living around. We have a name that is known."

She put a hand gently on his arm to stop him.

"Opio," she said, "you're half my life and I'm sure that what you say is true. I know it is. But also I'd not care if you were a fisherman's son with nothing in this world but three fishtraps and a net. Because I love you, Opio. But try and understand me in this matter, or rather the people I come from. You're not the son of a great household of the Baganda. That's all they'll know or care. And that'll be the end of it."

"We'll try that further," said Opio stubbornly. "I'll see your people tomorrow."

"Very well," replied Teri sadly. "You must see my uncle. He's the head of my household now that my father is dead. But it'll be as I've described."

The next day Opio went to see the uncle, who was called Ankole. He took shield and spear and his finest cowskin cloak and he stood before the man in the encampment near the Snake People's boats and looked as fine a figure of a young warrior as one would be likely to meet. Oronde came with him as a spokesman because it was not right that a man should make his own offer of marriage to the woman's family. Old Onyango should have done this, or Magere, but they were far away, and Oronde was a relative by marriage, and knew Opio's wealth and standing.

Ankole was an aging man, one who had once been powerful but was now shrinking into himself. His lips were thin and his nose curved like a beak and a kind of bitterness sat on the man. He accepted the beer and the sheep they had brought graciously enough, but carelessly too, as if it were no more than his right, and then he listened to all Oronde had to say. Oronde put it well and spoke with dignity.

When he had done Ankole was silent for so long that Opio wondered whether he had understood, or even heard. Even Oronde, who knew the pride of these men, grew impatient and thought to press the offer again. But when he began Ankole put his hand up for silence and began to speak.

To their amazement he was as mild as milk. Surprised at the offer, yes, though his dignity would not let this show overmuch, but obviously he saw no harm and had taken no offense. He knew Oronde's family and their wealth and importance and he trusted Oronde's report. Anyway, he could see with his own eyes that Opio was a man, and would make a worthy husband. Anyone could see that with half an eye. It was a pity his clan lived so far and that the marriage could not be discussed with them as it should be, but he understood the irregularity. There was even a faint smile here, and Ankole explained that he had once been young himself and not too long ago to know that haste was born of youth. It was, in a way, a compliment to his niece's beauty. In short he saw nothing against the marriage and much for it, since it would mean an alliance with a great Joluo clan.

Here he called for Teri and asked her gently if she wanted this marriage and she stood with downcast face and whispered that she did.

"Then we must discuss the bride-price," said Ankole with his thin smile, and at that Opio thanked him and went away exultantly with Teri, leaving Oronde and Ankole to haggle.

After that everything went as merrily as a woman putting on bangles for a dance. There had to be some little haste, Ankole said apologetically, for he and his people would leave for the islands shortly. It could not be delayed for the rains were due and the lake would grow dangerous then. The bride-price had to be paid in sheep and goats and skins, for cattle could not be taken to the islands in the narrow boats. Because of this the Snake People kept no cattle. All this Oronde was glad to advance Opio, and in two days it was paid and all the bride's people feasted at Oronde's household and celebrated the last day of the bride with her own people. Opio saw little of Teri these days, for since the dowry had been paid it was not seemly they should be together until she came to him as a wife, but when they did meet she seemed full of a puzzled kind of happiness. At the feast she was silent and withdrawn, as was suitable for the occasion.

On the following day Opio rose with the dawn. He dressed carefully, and then, with Oronde, he went to Mundere to fetch his bride. They followed the coast and a brisk breeze whipped their kilts about their knees and the sky was full of towering clouds. The rains were near and men's lives stirring toward their promise and Opio's heart bursting with happiness.

When they reached the shore where the Snake People had lived all these weeks it was empty. The shelters they had built were pulled down and the ground was scattered with abandoned posts. The thatch blew about the sand and some of it floated sodden in the water. The boats had gone.

Far out on the lake were three specks of canoes, but whether they were those of the Island People, or only Samia fishermen, it was too far to know. The Snake People had gone, Teri with them, and Opio knew in his heart that they had gone forever.

Then such a fury came over him as he had never known before and he cursed their cheating, black-heartedness, and the woman's too.

"You don't know she was part of it," said Oronde. "They may have taken her by force."

"She knew," said Opio. "A daughter of her people, if ever there was one."

Then they turned to go back to Sakwa and Oronde respected Opio's grief and anger and was silent.

But as they made their way through the market an old

woman selling dried fish clutched at Opio's cloak and asked, "Are you the one they call Opio the Fish?"

"No," said Opio. "I'm the one they'll call Opio the Fool."

"Opio the Fish or Fool," said the old dame, "it's all one to me. But if you're the man I mentioned then I've a message for you."

"Let's have it," replied Opio grimly.

"It's from one of the Snake People," she said. "A young girl she was, and pretty too, or would've been if she hadn't been a'crying. Girls are always crying and they shouldn't if they want to keep their looks and get good husbands. Never learn, they don't. However, she said to tell Opio the Fish, if I saw him, that it was none of her doing. None of her doing, she said, though what she meant by it is more than I can say. Girls' foolishness, no doubt, and maybe young men's too, eh? (here she looked severely at Opio). But none of her doing it was, and she gave me this."

And she held up a handsome cowrie.

Opio stared down at her. Then, "Bless you, Mother!" he cried, and he took her by the shoulders and danced with her in the market place.

"Eh!" she squawked. "Take your hands off me, d'you hear! The impudence!" and she beat him hard with a dried and stinking fish.

Then Opio took off the fine skin that he wore, a red-and-white skin covered in soft bull curls and without one blemish, and he wrapped it round her shriveled shoulders and left her.

She stood staring after him.

"Impudence," she muttered, and smoothed her hand over the skin, "though a fine young man for all that."

Then she moved her arms in the soft cloak and smiled and looked twenty years younger.

9

When they were at home and the curiosity, the questions and anger of the Owiti clan had been allowed to rage, Opio said to Oronde, "How can I get to the islands?"

Oronde sat down beside his friend and sighed.

"You can't," he replied. "You can't because no man here knows the way or could make the voyage. A Samia might, but when he knew why you wanted to go he would refuse to have any part in it because even the Samia are no fonder of a cut throat or spear in the back than anyone else. And, anyway, in a week the rains will begin and then men pull the boats up and dig their gardens. A canoe won't live in the storms that come at the beginning of the rains. So, you can't, Opio."

They sat in silence for a moment.

Oronde added gently: "There are other girls, Opio. Forget this one if you want to live to have grandchildren. You've lost the sheep but a long life is cheap at the price."

"I care nothing for the sheep," said Opio, and there was another, long silence.

After a while Oronde said: "Let me leave you now, Opio. The hurt will grow less."

Opio stopped him.

"No, don't go," he said. "I need your help. Tell me, do you know of any Samia who'd go? After the rains, if needs be. I'd pay high. Ten or twenty cows. Surely there are men who'd take a chance, even a big chance, for that, aren't there?"

Oronde sat down again and groaned. He explained how impossible it was. He said it in twenty ways and found new reasons why it could not be done as he went along. When he had finished Opio looked at him and said simply that he could raise thirty cows if pressed.

Then Oronde saw the hurt in his friend's eyes and cursed and went out to talk with the Samia.

After a week he found two men. Their names were Ojwang and Wanjala. They called themselves fishermen, but Oronde knew a better name for what they were. Both of them by birth Samia, they had lived most of their lives in the islands off the Uganda coast. They explained that they had come home to rest from their labors, whatever these were, but there was also a report of a missing boat and its owner. The story was vague as they told it and their own part one of wronged innocence, but, listening, one had a glimpse of lives which were one long history of troubles and moving on. They were both strong and capable men and said to be skilled boatmen.

Oronde thought that they would be dangerous in a fight. He was also of the opinion that they were as trustworthy as snakes, but said that if the price was made high enough, and a condition of their getting it success in what Opio wanted them to do, then they might be relied upon.

They demanded twenty good cows to be paid on their return. Also they would not sail until the first fury of the rains was spent. Opio accepted the price at once and Oronde moaned with pain when he did so. He had a decent Joluo sense of thrift. Opio swore to the bargain on his spear blade (May this blade kill me if I break this oath) and Oronde swore as witness.

Then there was nothing more to be done until the Samia thought it safe to sail.

Opio went home to Kano and told his family of his plans. His mother wailed, but Magere only said: "It's no use me or anyone else saying that this thing should either be done or not done. One can argue with a man, sometimes. But never with a girl, unless it's done with a stick. This one isn't within reach to argue with in that way."

"The choice is mine, not the girl's," said Opio a little stiffly.

Magere shook his head.

"No," he said. "It's not yours. It's the woman's through you. She leaves a message with a fishwife and hopes. That's a woman's way for you. But there, it's no use talking about it. Go with luck and try and come back. And do that soon, before the end of the rains, because I smell trouble with the Nandi. They'll be fighting before the year's out and we'll need your spear."

Two days later Opio prepared to go back to Sakwa.

Old Onyango happened on him when he was tightening

the thongs of a skin bundle of food and gear. Shield, spear and simi lay near on the ground. The old man looked at them with amazement.

"Are you going away again?" he asked.

"Yes, Father."

"But you've only just got back."

"Father, I explained it all to you."

"You couldn't have," said the old man.

Opio told him again of Teri, whom he had met in the market and married. Onyango listened carefully. He was getting very old now and news did not stay with him easily. He had forgotten but would never admit it.

"Where is this place? These islands? And how do you get there?"

When Opio explained he shook his head in dismay.

"I don't understand it," he said. "I simply don't understand anything any more. You say you want a wife. That's all right, very natural, but why risk your life in a boat going to the end of the earth to get one? There are girls in Sakwa, girls in Gem. Plenty of 'em. Alego, Ukwala, Kisumu too. All anxious to get married. But no, that's too simple for you. Going to an island beyond the sight of man. Perhaps it doesn't even exist."

"Teri was real," said Opio. "I know that."

Onyango was not to be brushed off with this.

"How can you tell?" he asked. "How do you know she wasn't a witch and vanished the moment you were out of sight, eh? No, don't tell me."

He silenced the indignant Opio with a wave of his hand and went on:

"People are beyond my understanding, these days. Once upon a time we were peaceful and stayed at home except for marrying girls in Alego and Sakwa or . . . Sakwa. I broke that stone pipe of mine there," he said gloomily. "Never got another like it. The finest one I ever . . . What was I saying? Ah, yes. Always gadding about. What in the name of Gogo are we turning into? Baboons? Apes that can never keep still? And fighting, always fighting. It's my brother's fault. A restless man, never still. Partly mine too, I suppose. I should never have gone on that visit to No. That's when it all began, while I was away."

"We don't lose cattle any more, Father," said Opio. "And we sleep safely at night."

"Yes," said Onyango, "and we didn't lose men then, either. Fifty, a hundred men I've not seen come back these last ten years. Which is more important, eh? Ah, well, I'm going to sleep. I hope you get your girl, Opio. I hope I'm here when you get back. Only hope so, mind you, I don't know that I *will* be."

He suddenly glared at his son.

"I don't know that I *want* to be," he said.

He shuffled off to his stool under the hut eaves. Opio looked after him affectionately. Onyango was getting very old.

He finished tightening the thongs and when the bundle was ready shouldered it. Then with spear, shield and simi he set out for Sakwa.

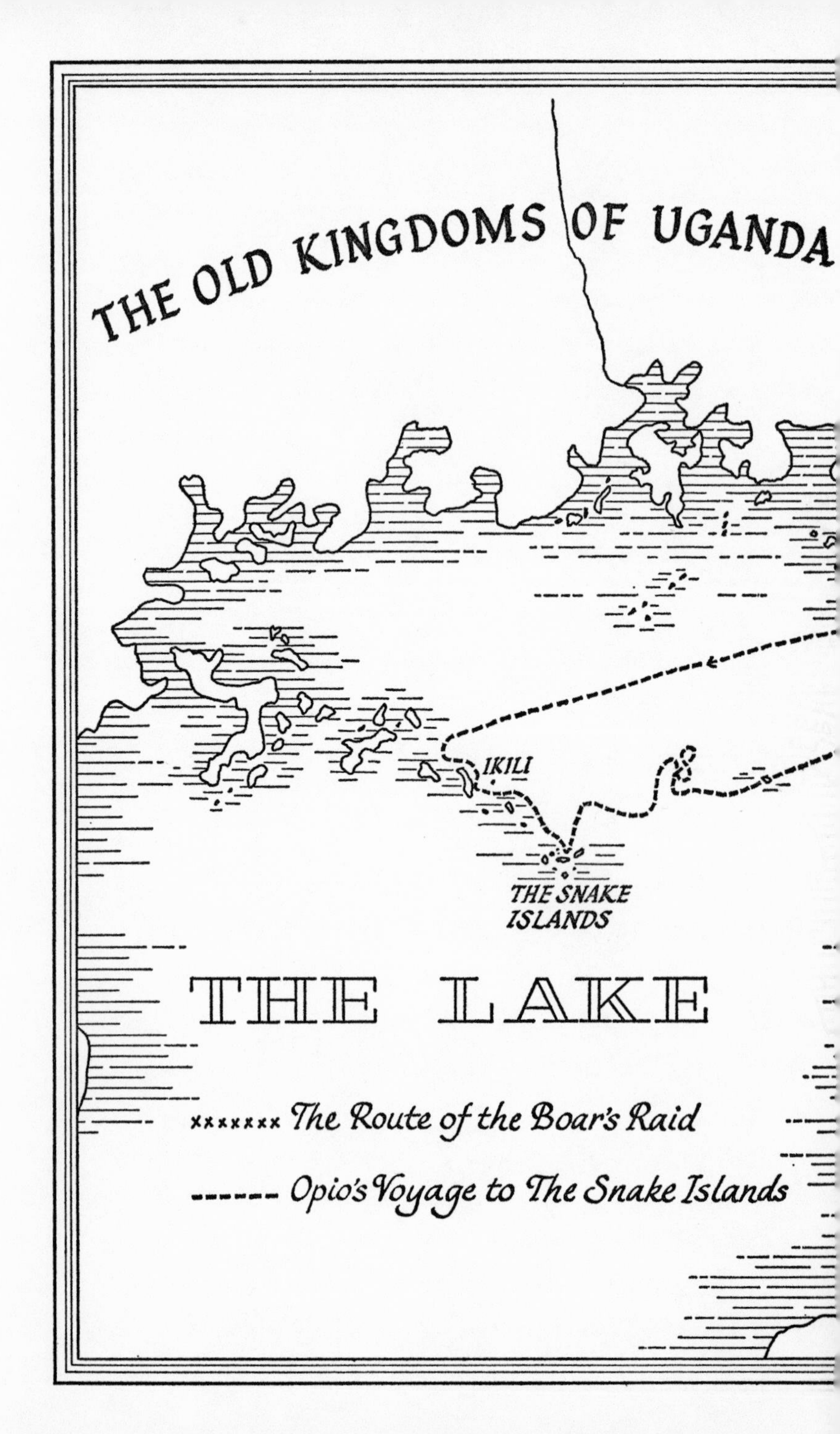
THE OLD KINGDOMS OF UGANDA
IKILI
THE SNAKE ISLANDS
THE LAKE
xxxxxxx The Route of the Boar's Raid
------ Opio's Voyage to The Snake Islands

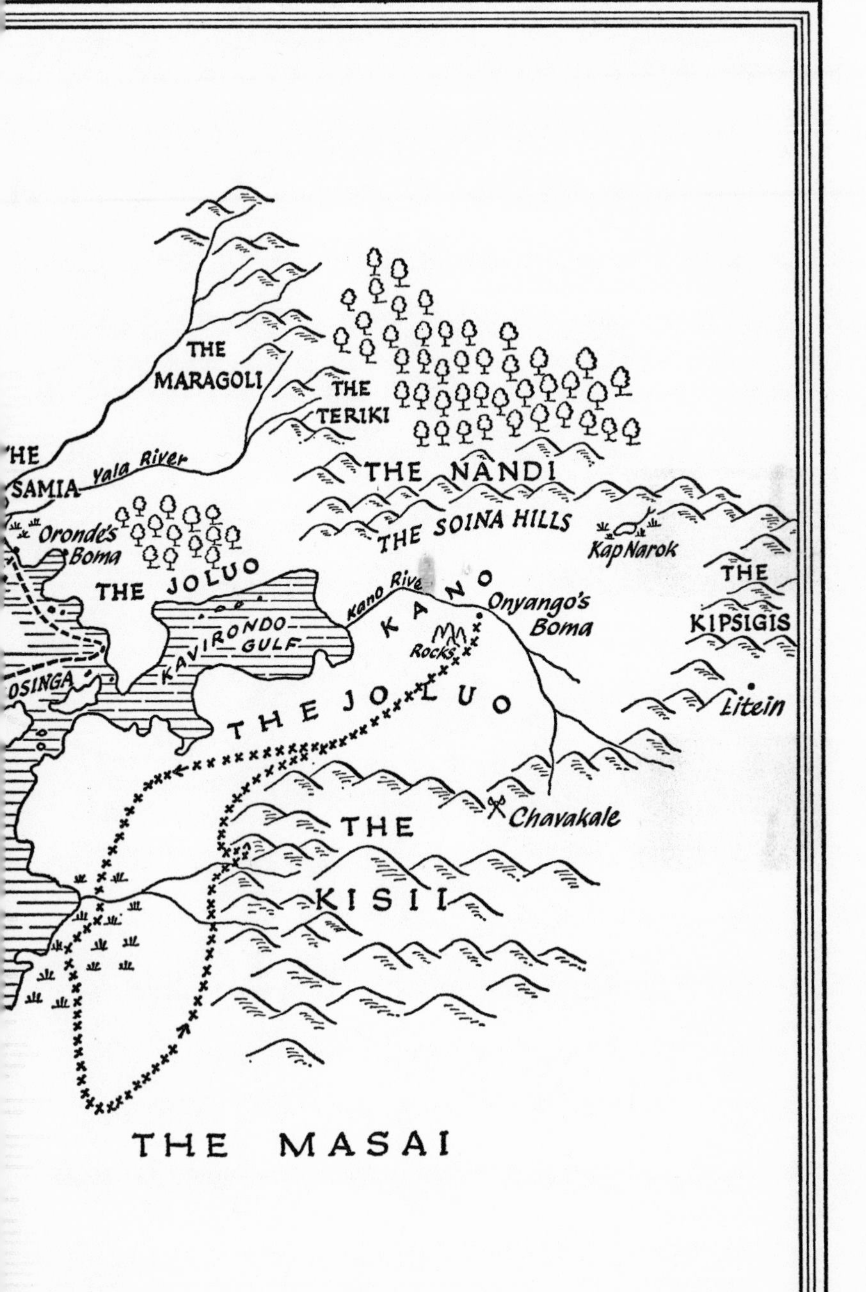
THE MARAGOLI
THE TERIKI
THE NANDI
HE SAMIA
Yala River
Oronde's Boma
THE SOINA HILLS
Kap Narok
THE JOLUO
THE KIPSIGIS
Kano Rive
KANO
Onyango's Boma
KAVIRONDO GULF
Rocks
OSINGA
THE JOLUO
Litein
Chavakale
THE KISII
THE MASAI

10

They sailed a month later at evening with the fisherman's wind.

At this time of the year it got up as the sun went down and blew steadily off shore most of the night. At dawn it dropped. The fishermen used their matting sails to take them to the shallow fishing grounds beyond the inshore islands, or at the mouth of the Gulf. In the morning they paddled home unless they were lucky with a freak breeze.

The voyage began in company with the Samia fishing fleet, but when, hours later, each canoe lowered its single sail and the torches were lit that would draw the fish, Opio's boat held on into the darkness of the lake. For hour after hour, until the glare on the water of the oil-soaked torches dwindled first to stars and eventually vanished. Then there was nothing but the shuffling feet of waves against the sides, the sail's rustling and the starlit immensity of sky.

He was wakeful. Unaccustomed to boats, he had been prepared for things to be strenuous and busy, for anything but this idleness. Ojwang drowsed over the steering paddle, often frankly asleep. Wanjala played a tune through his nose in the bows. Oronde was awake, for Oronde had chosen to come.

When Opio had returned to Sakwa he had found his friend short-tempered and gloomy. He had put this down to the trouble his affairs were causing. Then two days before the voyage was to begin Oronde had announced that he also was coming.

"It's not necessary," Opio had protested. "You've done all that kinship demands, and more. I'm grateful, but now you've done enough. This is my quarrel, mine alone."

"Nevertheless, I'm coming," said Oronde woodenly.

"Besides," continued Opio, "there's Andito to consider. You're newly married and I've no wish to make an enemy of my sister. This is no time to 'look for profit from your spear.' "

Oronde swore viciously.

"There's no profit to be got out of this raid," he said. "Nothing, unless perhaps a cut throat. But I'm coming and there's an end to it."

He grinned and added: "I've put sheep into the venture. I don't want them wasted."

There was indeed Andito to be considered, but not so much as Opio had feared. True, she spoke harshly to him, but, then, being a brother, he expected plain speaking and was not offended. She also kept a few of her complaints to share with Oronde. Then she wept. But Andito was expecting her first baby in a few months and her mind was too full of this to give her whole attention to the foolishness of her menfolk. All in all they escaped lightly.

So Oronde also sat in the gently swaying boat and grateful Opio was to have him there.

When morning came the land had vanished. The two Samia lowered the sail and lashed the clumsy roll it made across the two spars of the outrigger. Then they cooked maize meal on a small charcoal fire, the wood of the boat protected from the coals by a bed of hard clay plastered on its bottom. They shredded dried fish into the porridge, added rock salt and passed the mess in its hot clay pot up and down the narrow boat, each man taking a handful as it came to him, until the food was finished. Then they drank from the lake, and afterward took turns paddling, one man only working at a time, just keeping direction and way on the boat. Those who were idle slept. Ojwang and Wanjala on the bundled sail, their feet trailing in the water. Opio, who had been taught to paddle, watched the fresh of a wave, trapped in the outrigger, break over Ojwang and then run dripping from his chest. He never woke.

"Truly," said Opio to himself, "these men are half fish."

They were waiting for evening and the wind.

By later afternoon it was too hot for sleep. The Samia hoisted the sail again for shade only, there was no wind, and they all lowered themselves into the water to get cool and clean. Then Ojwang fished, for occupation mainly, for the lake here was too deep for fish, and as he did so Opio and Oronde asked questions about the islands of the Snake People.

Ojwang said that there were small uninhabited islands to be found everywhere in the lake, some of them little more than rocks where the birds rested. In this northern part they were scarce and difficult to find. If they had come on one this day they would have landed and slept there with the boat drawn up, but chancing on one was a matter of luck.

West were the great islands of the Uganda coast, some of them little kingdoms. These were fertile and the people on them thick as bees. At their southern end they thrust out into the lake in the shape of a great hooked arm, following each other in groups, growing smaller and further apart. The islands called Umfango, where the Snake People lived, were the finger tips of this arm, a lonely group. It would take at least three days to reach them, possibly more.

The navigation of the Samia was simple and dependent upon experience. They aimed their boat at a point midway along this arm, keeping westerly where they knew the islands to be close enough together for there to be no danger of passing beyond them without seeing land. When one was seen they would study its shape and know where they were. Then they would paddle east, always keeping islands in sight, until they came to the Umfango Group.

They had both been there a few times and described them. Five large islands, peopled and cultivated; a cloud of smaller ones upon which lived only snakes, crocodiles and fishing birds. They knew Ankole's clan and household, the greatest among the Snake People, although it did not hold the largest island. His huts stood at the top of a high red bluff, right above the water, and the gardens and banana groves of his clan covered every inch of land that could be tilled.

"Ankole is a great man," said Ojwang. "He's also a hard and bitter one. He won't be pleased to have his niece stolen."

"I'm not stealing his niece," said Opio indignantly. "I

married her. The bride-price is paid. I'm going to get my wife."

Ojwang yawned and scratched his great chest.

"Ankole will give it another name," he said. "But I meant no harm, friend. Cattle, boats or women. Earn 'em, steal 'em or marry 'em. It's all one to me, whatever you call it. I'm only anxious to get my hooks on the cattle we've agreed on. And to keep a whole skin."

Then the wind came across the lake. First in cats' paws that made the sail flap and the spar creak.

Presently it stopped playing with them and blew steadily.

They took four days to reach the Baganda Islands, for as they went deeper into the lake the wind grew less to be relied upon. On the last night it was calm and they paddled. Opio, who had warrior's hands, soft and unused to work of this kind, nursed sore and blistered palms by morning. The Samia grinned when he winced over taking up a paddle afresh. They did not suffer in this way.

By noon the first islands were seen and, as they went closer, recognized. Ojwang swore and complained that they had come further west than he intended. They paddled and slept in spells all the rest of that day, keeping each island, as it appeared out of the haze, well away to their right hand. There was no need to advertise their coming. They saw no other canoe and the Samia said there was little likelihood of doing so. The fishing was done at night and the only grounds worth working were far to the south.

At evening they edged in toward a long low smudge of land. Ojwang had been here years ago crocodile-hunting and said that although it was peopled the huts and gardens were at one end only. The eastern end was a desert of rocks and scrub where no crops would grow.

Opio, impatient to get on, asked why they should not move by night, as they had been doing, and Ojwang spat over the side and answered: "For the good reason that if we're to arrive I must make my way by sight. The islands lie wide apart here and if we get south of them in the dark we're in open lake. That's one reason. There's another and a better. Here the wind blows across and we must paddle and that being so I'd like my sleep at nights. I've no wish to argue with Ankole at the end of a sleepless night. I want my eyes open so that I can see what he's putting into the beer when he feasts us. Stick to your woman-stealing, Luo, and leave canoe work to me."

He wiped his face with a great fist and paddled on toward land. Opio grinned. He'd grown to like and even trust Ojwang, surly, rough-tongued and unscrupulous as he undoubtedly was. In some ways he reminded him of his Uncle Magere.

That night they ate their dried fish and porridge upon shore beside the stranded boat. They also built a fire to keep snakes and crocodiles away, for the island swarmed with both. A low sandy cliff above the narrow beach shielded them from inquisitive eyes.

Opio asked what the place was called and when they would reach the Umfango Islands.

"For your last question, I think tomorrow night. This place here is called Ikili," was the answer.

11

The island where Teri's people lived was large. A conical hill, regularly shaped and bald as a heap of grain, rose from its center and all around the base of this the land sloped gently to the water. The gardens were here, rich and carefully tended, the bananas grew tall and thick and there were clumps of a tall bushy palm which was new to Opio. Ojwang told him that the Snake People made good beer from its crown and that the tree came from Uganda. Beyond, there were four other main islands, a mile or so distant, but on the side from which Opio first saw it there were only small islets and rocks, all of them tangled over with cactus and aloes and a kind of creeping bramble with curved, vicious thorns. Empty and useless places, all of them.

On the closest of these to the shore the Samia beached the canoe at night. Having done so, they took out the mast and hauled the boat across a waste of broken pumice until it was hidden in scrub. Above where the boat lay they found a small hollow arched over with thorns, and when this had been cleared a little they carried to it the food and gear and weapons. Water they could get from the lake; food, if they did not wish to be seen, had to be eaten cold. The only way they could be found was by accident or by someone making a careful search.

From this hiding place at dawn, Ojwang had taken Opio and Oronde a minute's scramble through the thorns to where they could see the main island. It was near, within easy swimming distance, and, as Ojwang had described, there was the red bare earth of a bluff and above it a cluster of houses behind a towering hedge. The bluff fell to a small bay in which boats were drawn up and their loose gear stacked beside them on the sand. Opio looked long upon it and remembered Teri's words in the grove of trees at Mundere where she had spoken of her home. For, as she had said, all around was the great curve of the lake, freckled with waves and dancing light, stretching to the sky.

And then, as he watched, he saw three women, carrying pots upon their heads, leave the hedge about the huts and walk down steps cut in the bluff to the bay below. They stood the pots by the water's edge and bathed and their voices came high and clear across to the place where the men watched. Even words could be heard. Then, leaving the water, they wrapped their wet bark-cloth skirts more firmly round them, knotting ends at their waists, filled the pots and went back up the steps to the houses. One of them had worn red flowers in her hair, and they could see a blossom still floating on the lake.

And Opio knew, by her walk, that one of the women had been Teri, and his heart turned over within him.

Ojwang leered at him.

"Do we take just one or all three?" he asked. "There's room in the boat for three if we sit close. It'll be nice sitting close. They can help with the paddling too. And how's it to be done, Chieftain?"

Opio ignored him and looked at the scene across the water more carefully. To one side of the bay was a thicket of papyrus and water-canes. He studied it closely. It was the choked mouth of a small stream and the reeds ran unbroken to the water and there seemed to be no pathway running into it. And then he recalled something. After the girls had left the water and dressed, one of them had crossed to these reeds while the others had filled the pots. The reason why she had done this escaped him for a moment and then a memory of his mother filling waterpots at the river came to him and he saw why.

He pondered a moment and then he knew what must be done.

That night the two Samia were left with the boat and Opio and Oronde swam across the strait to the bay. The distance was nothing to either Opio, born beside the Kano River, or Oronde, with a childhood spent on the lake shore. The way was plain to see, for it was bright moonlight—too bright, in fact, for comfort. The danger was crocodiles, for although they were safe from them in the open lake where they were never found, it was possible that they might lurk in the shallow water between the islands. But they came to no misfortune and eventually crept dripping from the water and hid among the canes and reeds close to the bay. For weapons they carried simis, for these could be held in their teeth as they swam.

They curled like dogs in grass to make a hidden nest, keeping a screen of untrampled reeds between them and the open sand, and settled to wait out what remained of the night. It was a bad one, for they were eaten by mosquitoes and in the morning by great blood-sucking flies that bit like fire. They slapped at the flies and scratched and waited, Opio aching with impatience, Oronde cursing softly under his breath, but presently, as Opio had hoped, they saw the three women come down from the houses above to draw water. He had guessed it to be something that happened every morning, a household chore, and, as he had hoped, one of them was Teri.

The three left their pots upon the sand and bathed, and the men lay in the reeds and listened to them splashing and laughing.

"What next?" asked Oronde. "Go to them? There may well be folk watching from above."

"Wait," replied Opio. "One of them will come to us. The thing in question is which one. We may have all this to do over again."

Presently the women left the water and dressed and then they did the same thing that Opio had noticed done yesterday. While two of them filled the heavy pots one crossed the beach to the reeds, and, plucking a handful of them, began twisting and plaiting three small rings which would serve as cushions between their heads and the water-filled pots. And luck was with Opio, because the girl who came to the reeds this morning was Teri.

She stopped a pace from where they lay, twisted off a handful of feathered reed flowers, and began to plait. As she did so she sang softly and they could see the beads of water trapped in her hair. Then, with a dry mouth, Opio whispered her name. She did not hear the first time. The other girls were twenty paces away and if she screamed in fright there would be an end to it. He whispered again, louder.

She did give a tiny gasping cry and put her hand to her mouth, and then she recognized Opio and her eyes became wide. She stared and began, "But how . . . ?" Then she glanced at the girls wringing water from their wet skirts, turned her back on Opio and murmured, "Wait."

He could see her shoulders trembling, but her hands worked nimbly over the plaited rings.

Then one of her companions called, "Teri!" and she answered without a tremor in her voice, "Be patient, I'm coming," and walked away from the reeds.

They watched her speak to the girls and there was a little laughing argument whose words they could not hear. Then Teri helped lift the pots on the heads of the other women and they left her, walking erect, their bodies swaying gracefully to balance the loads.

"You mustn't be long," called one from the bluff, "for we can't begin without you," and Teri cried, "I'll be there in a moment."

Then she sat still beside her pot on the sand, with her hand plucking nervously at her skirt until they were out of sight. Then, after her eyes had searched the huts above, she walked to the reeds again a little above where she had made the plaits, gathered an armful, and went deeper into cover, dropped her reeds and was in Opio's arms.

Oronde watched them a moment and then rolled on his back and spoke speculatively to the sky.

"If you'll take the advice of a married man, and one, moreover, who is anxious to remain so," he said, "it might be as well to postpone this until a better time."

"He's quite right," said Teri. "Let me go, Opio. I cannot stay long if this is not to be talked about and, oh, Opio, you mustn't be seen here. Tell me what's to be done."

Then Opio spoke rapidly and she listened calmly.

Oronde and he would stay in the reeds that day. At night Oronde would swim back to the islet and bring the boat to the bay. Opio would wait for Teri. She must do nothing unusual all day and at night must go to her bed and lie awake until she was sure that all her household were asleep. Then she must come down to the bay and they would put what distance they could between them and the search that would follow.

"Can this be done, Teri?" asked Opio. "Or, first, let me ask another question. Do you want it to be done? If not, then you must go back and say nothing and forget us. Oronde and I will swim back to the boat tonight and there will be the end of it."

"I'll come, Opio," said Teri. "I'll come because you're the husband I chose and I only want you. If I stay I'll be married to some Baganda chieftain, greedy and old and smelling like a goat, with twenty other girls in his compound. And all to grease my uncle's ambition. That, when I could have you! But listen, Opio. I can't leave the household by the great entrance tonight, for it's always guarded. But there's a small goat tunnel through the hedge behind my hut. It's a path which leads down to a beach the other side of these reeds. I'll come that way and you must wait there. Bring the boat to that beach also, for it's safe and no one uses it. Here boats come and go, even at night."

And so it was agreed and Teri left them and took her waterpot and they watched her climb the steps, strong and graceful and proud, until she was gone beyond the crest of the bluff.

"Eh, love is wonderful," said Oronde, a full five minutes later. "He doesn't even feel the flies."

And with that he pointed out pleasurably a row of them feeding peacefully on Opio's shoulder. But it was quite true—he had not felt them bite.

12

When Teri had gone they wriggled through the reeds and found, on the other side, the small empty beach she had spoken of.

All that day they waited, one sleeping while the other

watched, but no one came near them. Nightfall, when it came, was clouded over from the south and there was a fitful wind. But the clouds were high and racing and there were moonlit spaces in which the beach stood open, still and empty.

Oronde put his simi between his teeth and walked into the lake, shivering a little as he did so. He waded silently until the water reached his waist and then lowered himself into it with only the smallest splash. Opio watched the dark head bobbing until it vanished and he was alone. He went up the beach and found the track that led to the goat tunnel in the hedge above. Evidently it was rarely used, for it was very faint and overgrown with weeds.

Where the slope steepened, the track changed to rain-blurred steps cut in the earth and at the first of these Opio waited. The bluff sheltered him from the wind and the night was very quiet. Once he heard men's voices from the other side of the reeds, and also, from above, the sound of an iron tool cutting wood. Later a night bird flew above him with heavy, beating wings and landed stiff-legged at the water's edge. He could see its curved beak and bobbing head as it ran dabbling in the last dying wash of the waves. It was drinking. Then it gave three harsh cries and struggled into the air again. He saw the hanging legs drawn up before it vanished.

Many hours passed and no one came down the path.

Then he heard the faint creak of a boat coming from the direction of the islet.

Still Teri did not come, and Opio despaired.

He went down to the water's edge and crouched beneath

a clump of sedge until the boat grounded with a soft hiss in the mud. There were three figures in it and the giant shoulders and tangled mop of hair of the man in the bows could only be Ojwang. Opio walked forward and helped to hold the boat while the three jumped ashore.

Oronde came to him and stared around.

"She's not come," he said.

"Yes," agreed Opio, "she's not come. Wait."

He stepped into the boat and walked to the stern where the weapons lay in a heap. He thrust the simi he carried into the hide kilt which was all he wore, found his shield and spear and took them up. When he returned to the beach Oronde looked at them and said, "You're going up?"

"Oh, yes," answered Opio.

"I don't think that would be wise," said Oronde slowly. "What, after all, do we know of this woman except that she makes plans which never seem to come to fruit? This is the second."

"Wise or not," said Opio, "I'm going up there—no, don't say anything more, Oronde, my mind's made up. Listen. Stay here, all of you, and give me enough time to reach the houses, more to bargain a little and return. Wait for that. If I don't return then wait longer if you wish to, but go while enough of the night remains to get from sight of land before daylight. But whatever you do, don't come after me. If you hear fighting above give me time to strike a blow or so and run here before you launch the boat. And be ready to welcome anyone that follows me. But if I don't come, then go."

Then he left them and went swiftly up the path.

It was steep and he blew a little before the top, for days of idleness in the boat had eaten away his wind. At the top the great hedge towered above his head, solid as thatch and thick as a hut. He crept along it and found the entrance to the tunnel, not as high as his waist and just wide enough for a man to lie in. He knelt and peered through and could see the other end like a small distant window. The tunnel could not be crawled in for the lowness of the roof, so he lay on his face, thrust shield and spear before him and hitched his body forward in jerks.

The night had been growing darker, but there was still moonlight between scudding clouds, and inside the tunnel, when his eyes grew used to it, he found that some light filtered through the matted stems. It came and went as he inched slowly forward. He fixed his eyes on the inner entrance and went on.

There was only a spear's length to go when it happened, a savage whisper in the darkness and a light blow on the shield pushed ahead. It hissed again and thudded against the hide while Opio wondered. Then knowledge swept over him and he gave a strangled cry and rolled back against the springy walls of the tunnel and the moonlight came flooding in and he saw it. A flat, evil, angular head curved back tautly, and beneath this the thick body vanishing into the ground. The eyes were cold and still.

Opio stared and his bowels shook and the sweat broke out all over him. It was a great puff adder, and, with his mind screaming, he wondered why, after two blows at his shield, it did not either come or go. Then he understood. The thing was buried halfway along the length of its body in hard-packed ground. It had been done by men. The Snake People. It could neither come nor go, only stay, angry and tormented, and strike at whoever came creeping along the tunnel.

Opio closed his eyes and the fury that swept up left him helpless for a moment. Then he grew determined. He put shield and spear to the ground, drew the simi from his waist, thrust it forward and saw the snake strike harmlessly again at the iron. Then the sharp blade swept across like a sickle, the lopped head fell to the ground, and the stump of body writhed.

He struck again and again until everything was still. Then he wiped the sweat from his eyes and lay panting. Presently he recovered, took up shield and spear and passed the horror, pressing himself hard against the wall.

He left the tunnel without caring if men were there or not. For a moment he stood in the shadow of the hedge, glaring at the houses looming in front, and beyond to where a fire burned beside the great entrance and men huddled before it, skin-wrapped shoulders hunched black against the glow. Teri had said that her house was nearest to the tunnel and he went to this one, moving like a cat. The doorway was beyond and he circled the wall, keeping clear of cooking pots and grain sieves stored beneath the eaves. The doorway was open and he breathed deeply and went in with spear up.

There was a low fire burning on stones in the middle

of the hut. Teri was lying on the floor at the far side and he thought at first that she was dead. Then he saw her legs and arms were tied with thongs and, when he bent to see, her eyes opened and stared. Then she began to sob and he cut the thongs with his spear blade.

He shook her by the shoulders and drew her up.

"Tell me," he said fiercely. "Tell me quickly and tell me the truth."

She checked her sobbing with an effort.

"How did you come alive?" she whispered. "The goat tunnel was . . ."

"Yes," he said grimly. "That trap's been sprung. Now tell me the rest."

"The boat was seen on Ikili," she said. "It was seen early in the morning leaving and sailing here. A canoe brought the news this evening and they found your tracks in the reeds and my staying behind on the beach this morning was remembered and I was questioned. Oh, Opio, they beat me. I told them nothing, but my uncle is shrewd and he knew. It was too late to search and they are short of men because many have gone to another island to feast. But they've sent for them and tomorrow they'll search. Believe me, Opio."

He was silent and she hurried on.

"They know you're here but not where you're hiding. What worries them most is that they don't know where the boat is. Meanwhile they blocked the tunnel as you saw"—she shuddered—"and watched the gate and, as you found, they made sure that I could not run away."

Opio looked at her upturned pleading face for a long time and believed her.

"Let's go now," he said gently, and helped her to her feet.

Nothing was moving outside the hut and they made for the tunnel entrance. Teri moved slowly, for the thongs and beating had left her stiff. She was kneeling to enter the tunnel when a man came suddenly round the hut behind them. He checked and exclaimed in amazement, then yelled to his fellows round the fire and came bounding forward with spear up.

"Go on," said Opio to Teri. "I'll follow when I've settled this jackal."

Then he turned and thrust his shield into the Snake Man's face, sending him reeling off balance. Opio stabbed and all his anger at past injuries was behind the blow.

Then he joined Teri outside the hedge and answered the question in her look.

"Your people owe me something," he said. "Now run for the boat and I'll follow. Be careful at the beach. Oronde and two others wait there and this commotion here will have made them quick to strike."

They ran down the steep path. There were steps behind them now, but they reached the bottom without trouble and found there Oronde and the Samia Wanjala, both armed and ready. Opio told Teri to run to the boat and when she had gone he turned to help his friends, but there was no need. A man appeared from the darkness, running, hesitated when he saw he had more than one to deal with, then cried to others above. Then he turned too late and went down before Oronde's spear, and they could hear the rest retreating up the path.

When they reached the boat, and had begun to push off, Opio looked about him and then asked, "Where's Ojwang?"

"He'd business on the other beach," answered Wanjala. "He'll come."

"It'd better be something he can do quickly," said Opio. "That crew above will return when they get their wits about them and know how few we are."

"Ojwang knows what he's doing," grunted Wanjala as he strained at the boat. "He's coming now, anyway."

The burly Samia came splashing through the reeds at a run. He was almost naked, carried a simi and his face and body gleamed with sweat. He drove the canoe into the water with one powerful thrust, flung a leg aboard and scrambled in. As they all took their places he laid down the simi to paddle and grinned at Opio.

"I see woman-stealing was a success," he said, glancing at Teri. "A pretty wench, I should say, though I'd need to see her in a better light to be certain. Possibly she's not looking her best. I hope she can hold a paddle. We'll need everything we can get in that direction."

"Where have you been, friend?" asked Opio. "You missed a little fighting here."

"I'm not sorry," said Ojwang, "for I've no love of the occupation. When it's well paid for or can't be helped, yes. Otherwise it's best avoided and I do so when possible. I've told you before, Luo, I'm a man of boats. I leave the fighting to others."

"Then why not stay by the boat?" asked Opio mildly.

"*All* boats interest me," said Ojwang. "For instance there were four fine ones drawn up on the beach beyond the reeds. I went to admire them. I put a hole in the bottom of each before I left," he added. "They were good boats and the wood was tough."

Opio stared at him open-mouthed.

"I never thought of that," he said.

"I keep on telling you," complained Ojwang. "When it's a matter of boats then I don't miss much."

By dawn they were almost out of sight of the island. The wind blew east across their path home, so they left the sail rolled and paddled. But when they had been at work in the daylight for an hour Ojwang looked back and then stood up to see the better.

"I thought as much," he said, and pointed.

There were canoes far away, at least ten of them. They paddled on silently and then after an hour looked back. The canoes were nearer and they knew that there must be many hands to paddle.

Ojwang and Wanjala put the sail up and the boat turned east and ran before the wind.

"It's somewhat off our course," remarked Ojwang, "but for my part anywhere is home as long as it's away from *those*."

13

When the course had been changed they sat and watched. After a pause the boats behind followed suit. Ten small shapeless sails struggled up, and then, as the wind took them, turned into tight bows. There was no mistake, these were the Snake People looking for vengeance.

Quarry and hunters now ran on a parallel course, the latter behind but edging in. The change had given them present gain but, as far as could be judged, all the canoes now made much the same speed. It needed time to show the truth of this.

Ojwang had the paddles brought in.

"Let's keep our breath. We may have to practice your trade, friend," he said to Opio.

After that they were silent and watched the boats behind while the sail creaked above and the water hissed below. By late afternoon there was no doubt left, the distance between was growing less. Now the men in them could be counted, sixty or more between the ten boats. Too many.

Ojwang was not cheerful but he was calm.

"They won't be up with us by nightfall at this rate," he said. "There'll be a moon, but too much cloud for it to matter. We'll try something then."

So they sat out the afternoon and evening, listening to the voices of the boat under sail, and saw the pursuing canoes grow black and sharp against the fading light. The sun went down and for a little space the world was bathed in a yellow glare before the shadows ran swiftly over the water.

When it was dark Ojwang bestirred himself.

"Now, friends," he said, "let's think in the language of boats. We must change course to one side or the other. They know we'll do this and will do likewise. If we go north we go toward our homes, if south, toward theirs. Now tell me, which side will they think we'll choose?"

"They'll expect us to go north," said Opio. "Go south."

"It's debatable," said Ojwang. "They may expect us to think they'll think that."

"Or," added Oronde, "they may expect us to think that they'll think we'll think that."

"It's too difficult for me," said Opio.

"Yes," said Ojwang. "The only comfort is that it'll be difficult for them too. I've always found it best at these times to leave it to luck. Let's do that. Wanjala, say the name of either a bird of the water or a bird of the land."

"A heron," said Wanjala.

"Good," replied Ojwang. "We turn north then, because that's the meaning I had in my mind to give to a bird of the water."

So softly they took the sail down, turned the boat and paddled north.

Hour after hour they went on, not speaking, ears pricked to the night around, the paddles gently dipping. They were hungry and low, for they had not eaten that day. There was, indeed, little left to eat, for the fish had been finished and only a handful or so of meal remained. Then suddenly Ojwang stood up in the bows and harshly whispered to them to be still. They all strained to discover what he had heard. There was nothing, only the water dripping from the hanging paddles. The wind had gone, the water dead calm. It was so hot they panted and the night was black and still.

Then they all heard the splash and dip of paddles.

Ojwang cursed gently.

"You should have chosen the other bird, Wanjala," he whispered.

"It was the luck," muttered Wanjala.

"Yes," said Ojwang, "it was only the luck."

They pointed the boat away from the sound, but as they were doing so the sky flared with distant lightning and a little wind came sighing across the lake from out of the darkness that followed the flash. It ruffled the water against the boat side, breathed hotly on their sweating bodies, then dropped.

In the brief flash they saw the Snake People's canoes, widely spread, close enough to see the paddles lifting. They also were seen, for there was a shout and another answering.

But Ojwang had lost interest in the Snake Folk. He exclaimed and stared into the darkness in the direction from which the lightning had flamed. When Opio began to speak he told him abruptly to shut up and listen.

Presently they all heard what he was listening for, a distant mutter of thunder and beneath it a deep steady note that grew louder.

"Leave those alone, friend," he said to Opio, who was groping in the bottom of the boat for the weapons. "There'll be no need to bother about the Snake People for a while. They'll have troubles of their own. Wanjala, get a corner of the sail up and the rest of you get those paddles in and tied down. The lake's going to take a hand in our affairs."

They had the sail up before the wind hit them, up, but rolled so that only a corner hung free. The moment it was done Wanjala flung himself out of the boat and across the outrigger, threw a bite of the grass rope that lay there round his waist, then gripped the spars with toes and hands. Ojwang brought the stern toward the wind with the steering paddle, braced his great legs straddlewise against the thwarts and bellowed to the rest to wedge their thighs beneath the worn logs on which they sat to paddle. Then the wind came like a giant, first hot, as though from a great fire, then icy. It whooped and howled and bent the mast and clutched them with huge hands.

The rain followed, solid and suffocating, and the boat filled beneath it. Ojwang screamed for them to bail and they got the sense from his contorted face, masklike in gouts of lightning, for the words were torn away and lost in chaos. They bailed with the half-gourds from which they ate, with the cooking pot, and later, when it had slipped from wet tired hands, with its broken shards. Finally they scooped at the water with cupped palms. They bailed, stopped to clutch the sides and seats when the tormented boat threatened to spew them out, then bailed again. The lake rose in great waves that came inboard with heavy smashing blows against their chests and sucked greedily at them going out.

They bailed; unthinking, uncaring, while the world erupted about them.

Once they stopped appalled, for in the light of a great flash they saw beside them a canoe. There it swung until it seemed to hang above them, bottom up, livid like the belly of an enormous fish, a pair of despairing hands clawing at a shattered outrigger, the man hidden beyond. They gaped and the lightning beat against their staring eyes, and then the boat was gone and Ojwang was cursing their idleness in the filth of a dozen languages gathered up and down the lake, and screaming for them to bail . . . bail . . . bail. . . .

Then they groaned and bent to work again and only longed to die and have done with it, if only Ojwang would let them.

Morning almost surprised them, a sickly light strained through ragged clouds when they had believed that it would never come again. The waves were still high, but the storm long past its worst. The boat lived.

They sat in silence with hanging heads, silent, that is, except for the chattering of their teeth. Inside the boat the water washed from bow to stern and back again. Wanjala had come inboard from the outrigger and joined the rest and Ojwang still cuddled the steering paddle, his eyes seemingly sunk into his head, naked body streaming with water.

There was still much fight in him, though, for at times he roused himself to curse or jeer at them.

"How d'you like my lake, Opio the Fish, eh? By Gogo, you look like one too; just gutted. But how d'you like her in a tantrum, the old bitch? And that reminds me, where are our friends of yesterday?"

He looked round at troubled water stretching to a torn sky.

It was empty.

"Hm," he said. "It seems their boatmanship was not as good as mine, or their luck perhaps. Well, well. Get that sail out a little, Wanjala, and let's move from here before their ghosts come to trouble us. And for pity's sake get the water bailed out, the rest of you. I could bear a dry seat."

The sun came out later that morning and comforted them, and also they found and landed on an island. It was a small, bare place that would be awash in bad weather, its rocks whitened and stinking with bird-droppings, alive with small green lake crabs that must have fed on feathers and other bird refuse, for there was nothing else. They hauled the boat up and emptied it and dried their clothes on the steaming rock. Ojwang and Wanjala fished, standing waist-deep in the water and using scraps of crab for bait, and they caught a string of very small lake perch. When the charcoal that remained was dry enough they cooked the fish, and these, with a little sodden maize-meal scraped from the bottom of the boat, gave them a mouthful or so to eat apiece.

"It's a poor way to begin married life," said Opio to

Teri. "I must try to do better for you when we're home in Kano."

But she smiled at him and replied, "I'm content."

They raised the mainland two days later, having stopped often to fish. They were far to the east of Sakwa and the shore was empty and desolate. They paddled west along it and at evening saw boats drawn up and a number of small shelters built beside them, so they went in to beg for food. There were six men there, Samia fishermen, drying their catch upon the sand. These, when they saw the boat coming in, got their spears ready and watched silently. As he stepped stiffly from the boat Opio realized that he and the rest must look an unlovely crew, lean and hungry and predacious as Masai cattle dogs. However, the fishermen recognized Ojwang and Wanjala and greeted them in a guarded way. When Ojwang explained their plight they gave them fish, a handful or so of green bananas and a little millet meal, and with this Teri cooked a meal in a borrowed pot.

They stayed there that night, making a fire somewhat apart from the fishermen. As they sat round it one of them came from their camp and joined Ojwang, bringing with him a pot of millet beer. The two of them drank and muttered together in their own language, and when Opio and the rest had laid down to sleep Ojwang went back with his acquaintance to the fisherman's fire and from there they could hear his great bellows of laughter. After a while Opio got up quietly and went to waken Oronde. He found him lying with his eyes open.

"I think it would be best if one of us stayed awake and watched, this night," said Opio.

"I'd that thought also," replied Oronde. "You watch now, and wake me later."

Then he turned over and closed his eyes and Opio went back to his skin and wrapped it round him and lay awake beside Teri, who slept quietly.

Much later he heard Ojwang return, a little unsteady on his feet and with a song grumbling in his throat. The Samia looked at the still shapes round the dying fire, swore a little and belched. Then he lay down on the sand and Opio heard him chuckle to himself and then sigh. Presently he was quiet and after that he snored.

When he judged it to be midnight Opio rolled across to Oronde and shook him until he got a drowsy answer. Then he went to sleep himself.

The morning was fine and when they went to the fisherman's camp to return the cooking pot everyone was still asleep. So they left the pot where it would be found and later launched the boat and sailed west. The Samia were stirring when they left and they shouted thanks and farewells to them, but got only a sullen silence in return. There was a light breeze and they used the sail. Ojwang seemed none the worse for his night's drinking and after a while looked at Opio with a twinkle in his eye.

"You seem tired this morning, Luo," he said. "You, Oronde, as well. Was sleep so hard to come by last night?"

Opio and Oronde looked at each other and then they grinned, shamefaced.

"No one trusts me," complained Ojwang pitifully. "I wonder why not?"

"It wasn't so much you as your company," remarked Opio.

"Ah, those!" said Ojwang, and spat over the side with disgust. "A dishonest lot. They offered me a share of your arms and gear if I'd help them cut your throats. It seemed too much bother for rusty spears and water-spoiled shields. I declined. They weren't going to kill Teri, though," he added, "so perhaps there's some good in them. One of them fancied her for a wife and was willing to give up his share of the gear for her."

"It's as well for them I didn't hear this," growled Opio.

"Why didn't you make the deal, Ojwang?" asked Oronde.

"I don't know," he replied, screwing his face up in thought. "Perhaps it was the deep love I bear for you both. Possibly the cows I have coming. I don't know. I'm a poor simple fisherman and sometimes it's very difficult for me to know what's best to do."

"I never met anyone who was less simple than you are," said Opio.

"Would you have helped cut our throats if it hadn't been for the cows?" asked Oronde.

"Oh," protested Ojwang, "you mustn't ask me that. That's a very difficult question to answer."

14

And that was how Opio brought his bride home to Kano.

She proved a good wife, skillful and quick-witted and mindful of her house gear, her gardens and, when they came, her children. And if in that inland place her heart sometimes ached a little for the lake, well, she was wise enough to know that one cannot have everything in this life. She had Opio and they loved each other and quarreled no more than is needed to add a little savor to the business of living.

Three years later (it was just after his second child had been born, a daughter whom they called Iteso) Opio, while visiting his relatives at Sakwa, went to the market at Mundere. And there, on the shore before a number of drawn-up boats, was a party of the Snake People. Among them was his wife's uncle, Ankole. He had grown far older than the three years that had passed, his hair was gray and he had begun to stoop.

Opio walked up to him and said, "Greetings, Uncle."

Ankole turned and after a moment recognized him.

"Ah," he said. "Opio the Jaluo." And then he smiled a thin smile and asked, "How is my niece Teri?"

"She's well," replied Opio. "We've two children now."

"Good," said Ankole. "Children are good. Well, it's pleasing to know that things go well with her."

Then he stared bleakly at Opio and added, "And with you."

He turned away, his sunken face looking hungry to the bone, and Opio marveled how much unfed ambition can waste a man.

Tapkesos

1

The trouble which Magere had expected from the Nandi did not come that year, after all, nor even the one following. But it came in the end and in this fashion.

The Nandi found themselves a leader, a man named Kilei. He was a formidable warrior, but there was more to him than just that. The Nandi had always possessed fine warriors in plenty; now they bred a man who could not only fight but also see a step or so ahead. Before him, the Nandi had always lived and fought in proud isolation, but Kilei thought wider. He looked for allies and he found his first in the slim fierce men of Chemelel, the Kipsigis. They were a people who spoke the same tongue and lived the same lives as the Nandi, but until now had shown little inclination to have anything to do with them. Kilei changed their minds. He went to Chemelel and spoke to a great council of the Kipsigis. Both, he said, were tribes of the same tribe, sons of the same father. They should help each other.

The Kipsigis listened dourly, for they were a cold people. Then they replied that if this was so then perhaps the Nandi would help them against their old enemies the Kisii, who stood in the way of their spreading south where the grass was good. And, greatly to their surprise, Kilei agreed, and promised to bring an army to Chemelel that year.

When the Kisii heard of it their anxiety overcame their dislike of the Joluo. They came to Magere with their fears and urged that both tribes should sink their differences and fight side by side against the threatened invasion. They argued their case with some cunning.

"*Now,*" they said, "the spear points at us. But if they win they'll take our hills, for it's country much like their own, only better. Then you'll have Nandi on one side of you and their brothers the Kipsigis on the other. At the moment the Nandi help them against us. But when we're finished Kilei will want payment. He'll ask for a little help in an enterprise dear to *his* heart. Perhaps you can guess what that'll be?"

Magere had been thinking much the same thing, so the upshot of it all was that the Kisii spokesmen returned home somewhat easier in their minds than they had been for some months, and later in the year almost five hundred Joluo followed them to Kisii.

Of the battle that followed there is no need to tell here in detail, for all battles are much the same except to those who fight them. Men survive and others die. Some do well and win fame, others better and their deeds escape notice. And memory usually improves upon performance.

It was fought in a deep lush valley called Chavakale,

beneath the brute bulk of the great Kisii Mountain, and was not a simple contest of strength and fortune where two armies clashed and fought it out, but, rather, a scattered botched affair, day long, where small parties stumbled on each other by chance and others hurried to assist. The Nandi and Kipsigis misjudged the nature of the country and by evening found themselves trapped beneath steep, creeper-covered cliffs in the eye of the valley. Some escaped by climbing, others by swimming under water down the narrow swift-flowing river that runs there, breathing, it was said, through hollow reed stems. When it was over, the Nandi and Kipsigis went home, those that still lived, and the Kisii kept their land.

Magere came home too, in triumph, for the Joluo share in the victory had not been small and after that nothing more was heard of the alliance between brothers, both on the side of those who won and those who lost. Perhaps the Joluo and Kisii ever afterward felt a little warmer in their feelings toward one another, and indeed there was a certain amount of marrying between the two peoples.

It was after Magere's return from the battle of Chavakale that old Adero, his mother, made a turmoil remarkable in power and endurance even for that embattled old woman.

She said (and her voice could be heard across the better part of three farms) that Magere should have done with traipsing about the world and must now get married.

Adero was now very old and looked as frail as a cobweb. She walked with difficulty and had at last to be content with ruling the household from a stool beside her hut doorway. But her eye remained as bright and quick as a bird's and her tongue matched it, and if the fame and importance of the greatest of her sons impressed her then she kept it a secret.

She said that he must have sons and daughters. What else was there to a man's life that made sense? she demanded scornfully, and then went on to answer her own question, pungently and at some length. The power of her tongue and endurance of her mind amazed even those who knew her best. And it dismayed Magere. Her complaints rumbled always and when all were convinced that at last she must be exhausted they would suddenly ride to new heights. Then those nearest would come running with tobacco and a hot ember for her pipe, or Teri's new baby to dandle, but anything to distract her mind and get a moment's peace.

Magere acquired a somewhat haunted way of staring round him and his hands an itchy habit of playing with his chin. As if he were longing for a new and splendid raid. Somewhere distant. Masai might do.

But it *was* strange to his people that he had never married, for children, land and stock are the three legs of the Joluo stool. And Magere was all a Jaluo.

Some said that it was the price he paid for the secret that kept him unharmed in battle. There was much wise wagging of heads over this about the fires at night. If no man could kill Magere, it was said, then to be sure he possessed a secret power. And it was certain that any such secret could not for long be kept from a wife. She would worm it out in a month and cackle it to the world when she drew water with other women at the river. And from there it would fly from tongue to tongue until the whole world knew. And once known, eventually, he would meet a man of his own strength in battle, and there would be the end of Magere.

And here the wiseacre would roll his eyes expressively and dispose of the man for his listeners by blowing an imaginary pinch of dust from the palm of his hand.

When Opio reported the tale his uncle bellowed with laughter.

"Secret!" he bawled. "What secrets have I got but this," and he bunched the great muscle in his arm, "or this?" and he tapped his forehead. "Let them babble. I don't marry because what use would I be to a woman with half my life spent carrying a spear far from home? This household has children enough with yours, Opio."

Here a thought seemed to strike him and he quailed and looked about him furtively.

"It would be as well, however," he muttered, "not to mention the matter to my mother."

2

One day, a year after the battle at Chavakale, a party of Nandi came down to Kano. They all looked to be old and important men, what could be seen of them for the great skin cloaks they wore, and they carried bunches of a flowering grass called *segutiet,* which was a sign that they came in peace. The people stared at them curiously and in silence, for very few of them had seen Nandi this close, except at the other end of a spear.

The visitors seemed not unsatisfied at the impression they made, but they asked, politely enough, if they might be allowed to speak to that great warrior Magere the Stone. So they were taken to where he was sitting outside his house, for he was a man who hated to be indoors during the day.

The old men squatted on the hard-beaten floor of the compound and laid their grasses down and, for all that it was a hot day, wrapped their heavy cloaks about them and looked as cold as snakes. Many men gathered there to hear what might be said: neighbors, and hangers-on who enjoyed Magere's meat and porridge, for he had plenty of that sort about him these days. Opio was there and an elder or two of the clan. There were many long ears that day.

Magere had beer brought for the visitors, which they accepted, sighing and coughing over it before their spokesman, who spoke Dholuo, thanked him and praised the brew. Then they drank heartily enough and made short work of a full pot or two before they had finished.

When they had done this, and the leader had made a number of polite inquiries about Magere's health and the cattle and crops, he worked his way to the matter he had come about, and, once started on it, talked at great length.

The Nandi he said were tired of war. Also there was a

famine in their land, and this, at least, was possibly true, for the rains had failed in the plains also that year. Worse than this, he went on, there had been sickness among the cattle. They foamed at the mouth and staggered and died and the best of their doctors could not drive the disease away. Times were bad for the Nandi. They had lost young men they could ill afford in the Kisii affair (as Magere possibly knew) and because of Luo raids the border people had left their lands to live with kinsfolk in the forest where they were safer. Eh! What with this and that and the shortage of food and cattle they were hard pressed and ready to consider anything that might ease their troubles.

The old Nandi sighed deeply.

Magere might perhaps wonder, he went on, why they were so frank about this to their enemies. But in simple truth it was forced on them.

"We're at the end of our tether and tired of useless fighting against a people as bold and able as you are. After all that's passed it will perhaps not be possible to be friends, but we'd be content with less, just with peace."

Here he paused and squinted up at Magere. Getting no reply, he coughed and moistened his lips with beer and then continued with another kind of tale.

There was in Nandi, he said, a girl called Tapkesos, the daughter of an important and powerful clan. She was thought by all that saw her to be as beautiful as the dawn. Beauty, of course, was pleasant, though nothing by itself, but truly this was a woman in a thousand, a graceful dancer, skilled at sewing and the curing of fine skins, at cooking and brewing. In this one it could be said that all the arts of a good wife were at her fingertips. Every young man was anxious to win her and there was no wonder at this. But here *was* an oddity. Pretty girls are usually fond enough of young men and eager to marry, but not Tapkesos. Rich the young men might be, and handsome and brave, all the virtues, but she never looked twice at one of them.

Now for some time her family had taken this to be the waywardness of a girl who knew herself to be beautiful enough to be able to choose, but as time passed, and one suitor after another was rejected, they became uneasy. Hints, and smiling tolerance, and a little natural pride at her fastidiousness had changed to frowns and then to blunt inquiry. They grew round with her, and at last, badgered beyond endurance, she had cried that she would only marry one man.

"Now here's another strange thing," said the old Nandi, leaning forward. "The husband her heart was set on was the greatest enemy her people possessed, a man of some repute here. She wanted Magere the Stone.

At this there was a stir of interest from all listening and the Nandi looked round with some pleasure at the effect his tale was having. But Magere smiled and asked, "What's this tale of a foolish girl to do with me?"

"It comes closer at the end," was the answer. "Let me go on. Now when the girl first blurted out her wish the family declared she was mad. To want to marry Magere! A Jaluo!"

Magere frowned a little. The scorn in the old man's voice hurt his pride somewhat.

"Made in its time and place perhaps the girl's wish was *unusual,*" he pointed out. "But was it so unreasonable? Am I not the kind of man who might turn a girl's heart? Even if she only knew of me by report. And to be a Jaluo these days, my friend, is no mean thing. If you don't know this your warriors do. The girl has my sympathy. She shows sense."

The old Nandi spread his hands and bowed his head.

"Forgive me," he said humbly. "We know what you say to be true. I only spoke of what the girl's family thought. May I go on now?"

Magere looked mollified and nodded.

"The girl was stubborn with her opinion and presently it seemed to her family that this was more than madness and worse. It was the blackest kind of treachery, and her father dealt with her harshly, but no beating would change her mind or break her spirit. Then, in a rage, he dragged her before the clan elders and demanded that they advise him as to what should be done with such a daughter. At first they also were filled with rage, but when questioned she spoke up boldly and they listened. Not as a father does but as men who must consider what is best for their tribe and clan. Their rage cooled and, like you, Magere, they found sense in what she said. Tapkesos had cried, 'If I, a Nandi, were to be married to the man my heart desires, then our two people might be joined and this war that wastes our countries at an end.'

"And indeed," said the old man gently, "we've come to believe it would be best."

There was a long silence.

Magere's face snowed his surprise and it was plain that for once he did not know how to reply. The story and the offer were slipped upon him so neatly that it took him unawares. It was foolish and yet not foolish, strange rather, and flattering too (he must beware of this), yet there was a rareness here that touched his heart. As perhaps it was meant to do. His mind hovered between pleasure and suspicion.

He temporized.

"This is something that cannot be decided in a moment," he began uncertainly. "It would have to be considered. Also you've told us about a wonder among women and your words were well chosen. But I can't forget they were words, only words. Every man praises his own. I'd have to see the girl before anything was decided."

"That's not difficult," said the Nandi, and his voice was suddenly as crisp and clear as that of a man half his age. Turning, he snapped his fingers and behind him one of the silent figures of his companions stood up and let a heavy skin drop to the earth. It had hidden a girl.

Magere stared at her in wonder. The old man had not lied. Tapkesos was beautiful.

Luo women can be handsome in a laughing comely way, and strong too, as they must be to work in the fields. But this was beauty of another kind altogether, and in Luo, Tapkesos would be a lily in a bean patch. She was slender, so slender it seemed a cruelty that she must support the heavy beads and bracelets that loaded her neck and arms. But she stood with all the grace and pride of her people and a loveliness all of her own. She did not smile, there was nothing about her which offered or begged or sought to win, but she looked gravely at Magere.

And Magere?

He fell in love with Tapkesos as finally as an egg is broken.

The old Nandi watched them both and his tired eyes warmed a little. Whether this was because of the wonder that was upon them, or at the success of his plan for their peoples, he did not say. Perhaps a little of both.

3

So Magere the Jaluo married Tapkesos the Nandi and there was peace at last. At least peace between the tribes, for there was little of it where Opio was.

Eh, what a wedding that was! And no easy matter to arrange for those whose duty it became. The customs of the two peoples were so different that they hardly knew where to begin. Old Onyango should have done it, but he was by now far too stiff in the legs and muddled in wits to undertake the work, so most of it fell on Opio, and a pretty time he had.

As for Magere, his mind was full of his bride and, there being no room for anything else, he was as useless as a bow with a broken string. When they asked his advice he bellowed: "Get me married, d'you hear? Just get me married and as soon as possible."

And when they complained of difficulties he bawled: "Difficulties? What difficulties? Since I've been old enough to notice, men have married girls all over Kano. I never saw any difficulty connected with it. I'm a man, aren't I? And Tapkesos looks like a girl to me. Then where, in the name of Gogo, is the difficulty? Have done with this babble and get us married. And soon. Do I have to teach you the ways of peace as well as war?"

And they said that Tapkesos was worse, though Opio had little to do with that side of the business, thank goodness, it being strictly women's work. But Teri complained bitterly. Before the marriage Tapkesos lived with her, and she and the other women tried to teach her how a young bride must bear herself in Luo, things which every chit of a girl had known without being told ever since she was old enough to stir the porridge. But it seemed that either she did not understand or she did not care. All she wanted to do was to marry Magere and not bother her head over the important business of *how* it was to be done. "But of course you will do that, Teri, won't you?" she said, and then they groaned and explained all over again, and worse, while they talked their heads off she smiled and looked more beautiful than it was right any girl should, and they wanted to spit. Eh!

There was another difficulty also, a most unexpected one.

Old Adero, who had cried so loudly and for so long

that her son should be married, now set her face just as stubbornly against it. While the plans went forward she railed and wept and would have no part in them. Her voice against it was edged and bitter to anyone who came near her, and then, when the day came, she stayed in her hut. And afterward she was changed, subdued and gentle in a way that those who had feared and loved her all their lives found to be most strange and sad. She no longer took any interest in household affairs. Only Teri's babies seemed to reach into the place where her mind had retreated and she was most content when they were left playing in her charge.

The day itself went off without misfortune. A great party of Kilei's clan came from Nandi dressed in their finery and the men of both clans sat down to the finest feast ever seen in Kano. It was true that at first they were silent and suspicious of each other, a little like dogs meeting, stiff-legged and hackles up, but the good food and beer cured that. The Nandi would have nothing to do with sound Joluo porridge, but they filled their stomachs with meat and had no complaint at all to make against the beer. Their liking for this might well have caused scandal, for when it began to rise in the heads of the young men of both tribes, and the boasting began, it was a good thing that the spears had been left outside. Indeed, as the night grew late, and noisier, some few went out to look for them. But Opio and a few other sober souls had thought of this and had collected and hidden the lot. So beyond a spilt pot or so, and one broken head, things went smoothly and the Nandi went home in the morning driving before them the bride-price of cattle, and walking with care because of their aching heads.

Magere married was a different man. He left the family hearth and built himself a great new household on land of his own, nearer to the river. There he lived with Tapkesos, surrounded by tenants and followers, and a great change came over him. He stayed at home and enjoyed his wealth and fame, took pleasure in the flowering of his millet and the boiling pot, as they say. Certainly he seemed content. Also he grew a little fat.

His people approved of the change, that is the solid, land-loving people of his clan. The rest who had been about him, the hungry sort, those whose tastes ran to fighting and feasting and little else, they either changed their ways with their master or looked for profit and excitement somewhere else.

Magere often came to the old household to talk with his mother, for this was one change that troubled him. He would sit by her stool with Opio's children playing at their feet and talk and never a mention of his marriage between them. And Opio would join them, for the two men were firm friends, more like brothers than uncle and nephew, for now that they were both married, and householders, the difference in their ages seemed less.

Only once, at a moment when Magere was about to leave, did Opio hear Adero speak of what lay between them.

She said: "It's foolish to want anything in this life because it's never given in the way one asks. I'm like the frogs who asked to be given peace and order and were sent Mamba the Crocodile."

"This is foolishness, Mother," said Magere gently. "There's no crocodile in my happiness."

"It's not foolishness, my son," replied Adero. "There is. You'll see. And I'm humble because the fault is mine."

Then Magere shook his head with a smile and looked fondly at his mother and went home.

4

Tapkesos always seemed as happy as she was beautiful, and Opio found this somewhat strange, because she was alone among women who would have torn her to pieces with their nails if they had dared. There were many girls who had wanted to marry Magere and yet he had looked for a wife elsewhere and found one among the Nandi. This seemed to them a bitter slight and the woman's beauty a worse one, and they only hit at her rather than him because it was easier and gave more satisfaction.

They showed their hatred in little things, by never staying to gossip when she went to the river for water and to bathe, by not exchanging trinkets or coming to her to borrow household gear. And they never gave her a pet name;

to them she was always simply the Nandi. Little things. They eat happiness as locusts grass. To do more would have been dangerous, because it was plain that to Magere she was the sun and the moon. And whether you were man or woman he was not one whom it was wise to make an enemy.

The only friendship shown her was by Teri. It may have been because they were both foreign, but between them was a little warmness. Also perhaps because Teri had not one unkind bone in her body.

So Tapkesos should have been a lonely woman, and therefore an unhappy one, but she seemed not to be so. She was entirely content with her husband and they were more constantly together than is usual with man and wife among the Joluo even when they are newly married. She loved to make him tell stories of his past battles, and, it must be said, Magere needed little encouragement to do this. Now the old kind of life was over he began to weary his friends with tales of his wars and they would sometimes have been grateful if he had talked of something else or, at least, told each tale fewer times. To endure him droning on often seemed a stiff price to pay for the beer he gave them, good as this was. But it seemed to please Tapkesos.

"Magere," she would say, "tell us again of that fight with my people, the one where your shield was lost and they all raged round and even then couldn't harm you."

Or another time when the talk was becoming spread about and enjoyable she cried, "Tell us how you fought the Masai, *Lekakeni*." Then Magere would plunge with more relish than art into some tale of slipping on wet stones in the Ingesi River during a fight and lying there helpless and yet nothing had put an end to him (or the tale). For the seventh time that month and all sighing inwardly and searching for strength to keep awake. All, that is, except Tapkesos, who clapped her hands and looked adoring and murmured, "How was that possible, Magere?" as the story bumbled on.

He had nothing of Opio's gift with a tale and was fast becoming a bore, as great warriors are inclined to do once their wars are over.

"He should have died in battle," declared a salty-tongued old man to Opio one night as they left the fire. "It would have been kinder to his reputation, and much kinder to me."

But there was never a complaint of this kind from Tapkesos.

"Eh," she would breathe, as the story came at last to an end, "what a man I've married! How right I was to follow where my dream led me! I wanted a man different from all others and I've found one."

Then she would look soft-eyed at him and say in wonder, "How can you have been so often in danger and yet never a scratch to show?" and move closer and rub her cheek on his shoulder and smile, and those watching would feel a pang that all this beauty was not for them. Then the softness would change to laughter and she would cry: "You've a secret! That's it. All the tales the old women tell are true. What's your secret, Magere?"

And Magere would snort with laughter and shout: "Secret? Yes. I've a secret. I was born in the year of a great wind and the witches gathered at my birth like crows round a dead ox and they gave me . . . Come closer, Tapkesos, and I'll whisper, for only you must know."

Then her head would bend gracefully toward him and with his mouth at her ear he would give one great bellow and she would clap both her hands there, all but deafened, and pout and indulgently watch him shake with laughter.

Then perhaps he would grow serious and say quietly: "I've no secret. I was just a warrior and could be one again if this life didn't suit me better. I was born to fight as others are born with the gift of magic, or that of story-telling, like Opio here. Tell us a story, Opio, and pass the beer, friends. I'm parched with talking."

5

Almost half a year after the marriage Oronde came up from Sakwa to visit his wife's people. He told them that the news of the lakeside people was so good it was not wise to talk about it. There was peace and a heavy harvest and Andito had a new son who was called Odongo.

Now it was the idle season and when Opio and Oronde had talked themselves out the days seemed long and flat and Opio searched for something to occupy their time and it occurred to him that a hunt would do that nicely. There was a small marshy lake under the hills far up the valley which the Nandi called Kap Narok and this was a famous place for pig and all kinds of buck and water-birds. It was wild and out of the way and very seldom visited and had a poor reputation among the timid because the springs which bubbled out along one shore were boiling hot and stank of sulphur. It was to Kap Narok that Opio set his heart upon going.

When the scheme was put to Oronde he was eager enough and also Magere was asked if he would come. Rather to Opio's surprise, for Magere was as home-loving as a weaver bird these days, his uncle welcomed the plan and rubbed his hands together with pleasure at the thought.

So one fine morning they set out. They took with them two grown boys, sons of Magere's tenants, to carry the food, and also a small pack of dogs.

They went north and west across the plain toward the blue hills, and the thorns were full of blossom and building birds, and Opio thought that he had never loved Kano so much. Magere also was happy and the sweat beaded his face as he walked, and presently he sang in a great voice and all about the dogs ran with noses down and tails up and the heavy ground-hornbills blundered into the air with indignant squawks.

They reached the lake at evening when the long shadows of the hills were already across the water. It lay quiet and dotted with fishing birds, and on the far shore steam from the hot springs drifted straight up into the still air. On the water was a small drift of flamingoes, pink and white, a rare sight, for they seldom came this far, but stayed beyond the hills on the bitter lakes of the Great Valley. A place where none of them had been but knew from story.

There was also something else, the smoke of a fire on the near shore, and at this they looked with distaste.

"Eh, others have the same idea," said Magere. "This is unlucky. The place is small and they'll spoil the hunting."

"Let's slip round and past them," suggested Opio, but his uncle said:

"No. We'll go down and find out who they are. If they're few perhaps we can make one hunt and do better. Sooner that than spoil both our chances."

So they went down and there were three young Nandi about the fire. Wary and silent they were at first, but when they learned they were speaking to Magere they looked at him curiously and one of the young men said, "My name is Kipsaina and I'm by way of being a kinsman of yours, for Tapkesos is a woman of my clan."

Then he welcomed them to the fire and presently Magere made soundings on the matter of hunting together.

"We didn't come here to hunt meat," said Kipsaina doubtfully. "As you can see, we brought no dogs. We came for flamingoes, for we prize the feathers and it's rarely that we have a chance to get them. A herdsman reported them on the Kap and we came in haste, afraid they'd be gone before we got here, for, as you know, their coming and going is a law that only the birds themselves understand. But the luck was with us, for here they still were and we've killed a dozen with our bows, and the feathers are as fine as ever I've seen. Look."

Here Kipsaina unwrapped a roll of skin and showed them a soft mass of feathers flaming in the evening light.

"However," he went on, "since we've finished what we came to do, what harm in staying a further day to hunt? We've only war-spears with us and they're somewhat heavy for the work, but we all have bows, though the birds' heads on them must be changed if they're to be used."

So that night they all ate together about the Nandi's fire, and later, when their stomachs were full, Magere brought forward a great stoppered gourd of strong beer. It was somewhat thick because of the carrying, but the day's walk, and good companionship, and the sparks from the fire going up in the night made it taste good, and soon they grew merry and liked each other as if there had been no difference between Nandi and Joluo in this world.

Next morning, before it was full light, the Nandi were about, busy unlashing the blunt heads of their arrows and replacing them with iron barbs. This done and all ready, they left the boys with the gear that they had no wish to carry and, cuffing and calling the dogs to order, went round the lake to the great field of reeds and elephant grass at the far end.

Dogs and men searched it all that morning but found only once, a duikerbuck which slipped away like a shadow, then broke from the reeds and scampered across the plain. In spite of calls, half the dogs followed frantically, returning only at noon, sore in the pads and heads hanging with shame. They drank deeply from the lake and then limped close to the men.

"This won't do," said Kipsaina.

But after noon, returning along the other shore, they saw pig. Five of them trotting from the thorn scrub across the cracked, dried mud of the lake's rim. The heavy, ugly, dangerous warthogs of Africa. The beasts lowered their heads and knelt to drink, and while they did so the three Nandi went wide through the bush to cut them off, and the Joluo went forward with the dogs.

Once they were seen it was heads and tails up in heavy scampering flight along the shore. Opio saw the little puffs of dust their trotters raised, the men racing among the thorns to his right, the dogs stretched to their uttermost effort before him, grunting at every bound. Then he put down his head and ran. Behind him the heavier Magere panted, but Oronde met disaster in a wet patch and vanished, sprawling, from the race.

The dogs outran and turned a boar. There was the whiplash sound of an arrow and it stumbled and wallowed, gored a too-reckless dog with a savage sideways slash and the rest held back, all frantic bark and no bite. Then the boar was on its feet again, angry, solid and dangerous. Magere and Opio both checked and the boar hesitated between them. Then it charged Opio, who flung his spear and missed by a length. He dodged and the boar went past, wheeling on Magere, who waited with narrowed eyes and then got home hard with his spear. He was still holding it off at shaft's length when Kipsaina killed it with an arrow at ten paces.

They gathered round, laughing and panting, all talking loudly and listening to no one. Presently they grew calmer but well satisfied with themselves.

"Eh!" said Magere, "but I'm more broken in the wind than a beer-maker's assistant. I'm growing old. Well done, Nandi. Opio, beat off those dogs or they'll leave us no meat."

They cut out the curved-edged tusks, for the Joluo value them as ornaments, then slung the carcass on spears and carried it to their camp. That night they feasted high on pork cut in strips and broiled across the fire and afterward they talked and sang, and Kipsaina told them of elephant hunts in the high forest of Kakamega, and of the great bear which lives there, huge and secret, of which it is believed that if a man but sees it once he pines and dies. Never were men more content with each other.

The night was strangely cold and mosquitoes came from the marsh in clouds and they slept badly. Every hour a man would rise sleepily, thrust fresh wood on the fire and then huddle his blanket skin closer, covering what he could from the insects. But toward morning the mosquitoes vanished and they all slept more soundly.

Opio awoke uneasily, wondering what had reached in through his sleep. Then he was suddenly alert.

The light was the grayness that comes before sunrise; the fire still smoldered feebly, buried beneath ashes. He listened and tried to remember why he should be uneasy. Then beyond the fire he heard the soft scrape of something heavy being dragged. When he raised head and shoulders carefully the noise stopped. Once again there was nothing but the world stirring toward morning.

Then there was a low, thunderous cough, like the first touching of a great drum and the player's hand flattened on the skin to kill the sound. Opio's scalp crawled. He yelled, leapt up and across a sleeping Nandi and kicked the heart from the fire with his bare feet. The sparks flew in a shower.

It was a leopard with the carcass of the boar. It gave a rumbling warning, seized the meat and ran toward the bush. Five bounds on, it paused to snatch a firmer grip and Opio flung a spear with all his might. It vanished in the blur of the moving beast, but the leopard screamed in full-throated hate, an appalling sound that plucked men helterskelter from their sleep. Then it was gone and the others gathered round Opio, questioning him fiercely.

They heard the noise again, round the far shore, a distant furious yell with a high note of pain. It was making for the reeds.

They ran up the shore and found the carcass of the pig. It was too dark to do more, so they returned and fed the fire high and warm. The light came in a little while and they again went out to the meat and spread out and searched, but there was no sign of Opio's spear. Presently Kipsaina called them and when they came he pointed down. A patch of leaves gleamed and they followed his pointing hand to where a bright chain of scarlet beads caught the light.

"He bleeds," said Kipsaina. "Your spear hangs in him, Opio, and we'll follow as easily as a man finds the path to his own mouth."

Then they returned again to the fire and ate a little of what remained of the cooked meat. A leopard hunt is not something to be rushed into on an empty stomach.

When that was done they began to follow the blood trail, all of them cautious, serious and silent. The dogs hung back, slinking behind with flattened ears. They did not like the tale their noses told them, were torn between their fear of going forward and that of losing the men. Opio was disconsolate. His spear was gone and he felt useless. He carried a borrowed simi. Kipsaina had a shield and was the only man with one.

The leopard had kept to the bush and made a great circle round the lake. The dusty blood drops lay in an almost continuous chain and were easy to follow. It had bled badly. Then they grew less frequent and finally vanished. At first there were still rare smears where the beast had scraped a branch, but soon there was no more blood and they followed signs more subtle. But there was no difficulty; the dragged spear broke twigs and bruised leaves to one side and the pain and anger made the leopard careless.

They were beyond the lake's far end now and had passed the reed bed. They thought at first it was making for the hills, but abruptly, on the bank of a small stream, it had turned back, following down the course.

They found where it had paused to try to get rid of the spear, turning like a dog in straw, attempting to bite the shaft.

"You took him high up and behind the left shoulder, Opio," said Magere, bending over the signs. "It's a difficult place for him to bite and yet he limps. Look there, he leaped and yet landed on three feet only."

Later it had rolled in ferns and gone berserk, for bitten

stalks and raked clods lay scattered. The wound had bled again.

Then one of the Nandi bent and grasped something at his feet.

"Eh! Opio!" he called. "Here's something of yours."

He held up a hunting spear, which Opio took gratefully and examined. The blade was smeared with drying blood and the black hard wood gashed with teeth marks, but it was sound. Opio smoothed a hand down the shaft and cleaned the blade in gravel. Then he straightened and grinned.

"He's given me back my teeth," he said.

After losing the spear the leopard had gone to the stream and drunk. The pug-marks were plain in the mud at the edge and there were threads of scarlet waving from the water-weeds. Then, freshened but still limping, it had moved with resolution, as if to leave pain behind. Straight for the reeds at the stream's mouth the marks led, and a little later they stood before a great dry clump of these and heard within the same great rumbling threat which had begun the business that morning.

They were silent and wiped the sweat from their faces. The hunt was at an end and only the kill to make.

While they waited and considered, the leopard shifted to another clump beyond. It was vivid in the sunlight for a moment and then the reeds took it again. When they edged nearer it yelled defiance from its hiding place and afterward was silent.

They all knew what to do and went soberly about it without debate. One of the Nandi took a drill from a pouch and made a small fire. When it burned up they took reed-stumps for brands and fired the reeds beyond and to each side of the clump that hid the leopard. Then they hung back a little with spears ready and waited.

It did not keep them long. It came out wearily and stood in the sunlight eying the smoking chaos about. The reeds crackled and smoke drifted into the men's faces. The leopard turned its yellow and lazy eyes on the front and considered the silent men.

Magere moved forward, but Kipsaina said quietly: "No, Magere, I have the shield. Stay to one side and make the kill."

The leopard blinked at the movement and the hatred bubbled again in its throat. Then, bending its head carelessly, as if it meant to lick a flank, without pause it launched straight at them. Kipsaina's shield took the weight and he staggered. One forepaw clawed at the top edge and the great hind feet came forward and up to rip. Then Magere stabbed at the throat and the rest closed in round the huddle of shield, man and beast.

When it was over they pulled the dead leopard off the shield and Kipsaina rolled clear. They all stood in a circle, looking down, awed.

"When one is great the spears come from all sides," remarked Oronde.

"Eh," said Kipsaina, "but he was brave!"

"You didn't do so badly in that direction yourself, Nandi," said Magere.

6

It was after the hunt that Magere fell ill.

During the whole of their journey back he was silent and seemed saddened. Once he said to Opio, "Eh, but it was a good hunt and that Nandi kinsman of my wife's a man to warm your heart." But for the most of the walk he was silent and when he reached his hut he staggered as if from weariness.

The next day he was too ill to walk.

Tapkesos nursed him skillfully, making medicines from plants and fruit, for Nandi women are often skilled herb wives, but Magere's trouble was beyond her simple knowledge. Then Joluo witch doctors were sent for, the white sort, who use spells and skills for good, not evil. They came from No and Kisumu and were given cows to pay them for their trouble and in exchange they lavished out their strange medicines and even stranger spells. But it was all wasted. They looked at the sunken face of the man on the bed and all of them returned to their places puzzled and not at all anxious to talk of the matter. For it does no good to the reputation of a doctor when a man as well known as Magere dies in his care.

And people had already begun to whisper that he would die.

Then Tapkesos cried out that there was only one man who could cure him, an old doctor of her people who lived at a place called Litein beyond the hills. He must be fetched, she said, and at once, no matter if it cost every beast they owned. The clan murmured doubtfully and asked whether any man could do better than their own doctors, and at that the gentle Tapkesos screamed at them and tore her clothes. So her husband was to die because Joluo valued cows more than men!

Someone came to fetch Opio and he went and found her a demented woman and the others silent and sullen. They were angry because she was a Nandi, because she called them skinflints and, most, because she was beautiful. And her accusation hurt them all the more because there was a grain of truth in it. They are a people who hate to waste good stock on sickness, which comes from nowhere and must be accepted.

Opio listened to everything. When he had done so he took Tapkesos' side and sent word to the Nandi asking for their help in getting the doctor she demanded.

He was called Arap Bet and it was true that his fame was great and known even beyond his own tribe. He came three days later and it was a wonder to everyone that Magere had lived that long, for you could see death in his face.

The Nandi was an old man who had once been tall but now stooped. He was as lean as a stork, with hot eyes and a gray beard, and he wore a leather cap, black with age, from which drooped the bright tail-feathers of a forest bird. He stood looking down at the sick man and heard out all that Tapkesos had to say, for the old man spoke no Dholuo. Then he motioned back the curious who pressed in the doorway, and with only Tapkesos and Opio and a few old women to watch, he set to work.

He unpacked the skin bundle that had come with him and took out the tools of his trade: green snail-shells strung on the wirelike hair from an elephant's ear, five curved rams' horns filled with a powder that smelt of spice, and a gray monkey's tail. Lastly a thin keen knife scratched all down the blade with a pattern fine as that found on the wings of a dragonfly, come perhaps to that inland place from some long-dead Arab of the coast.

Then he began his magic.

"A master among magicians," said the old women whose self-appointed task it was to watch at deathbeds, and they sucked their pipes and watched each move with greedy eyes.

The spells he said were in an unknown tongue, perhaps that of the Serikwa who dug the round pits found in the Nandi Hills and then vanished, no man knows where. He flourished the monkey's tail in all the dark corners of the room and then bent to tie snail-shells round Magere's wrists, ankles and neck. The rams' horns were laid at feet and shoulders and head, and then, taking up the knife, he lifted a limp arm and made a small cut.

When he had done this the awed watchers heard him exclaim and mutter in his own tongue. Tapkesos seemed to catch the words and start and bend forward. Opio saw nothing strange. The cut was a merest nick of the skin, it did not even bleed.

The cure went on. Arap Bet took ash from each of the horns and rubbed this in the cut. Then he sat at Magere's feet and seemed to sleep while the rest waited and the house grew dark and hot. At last the magician stirred. He looked keenly at the still man on the bed and then told Tapkesos to wash her husband in warm water mixed with a little fine-powdered charcoal. When this had been done to his satisfaction he demanded food and a place to sleep. In two days, he said, they would know if his arts had worked. There was nothing else to do but to wait. Meanwhile he was an old man who had traveled far and fast and these days he found that the practice of his magic tired him.

But Magere did not get better. He tossed and muttered on the bed, now burning hot and running with sweat, now pierced and shaking with cold. Worst of all, he ate nothing, only drank a little of the milk Tapkesos gave him, and by the end of the two days not even that. By then he lay speechless, not recognizing his friends or his wife. Arap Bet shook his head and confessed the sickness to be beyond him. He refused payment and took his skin bundle back to the hills.

That night the women who lived near began to wail and scream of Magere's life and deeds to the darkness around, as was the custom when a great man lay dying. Opio stayed with Tapkesos and the sick man until he heard the women keening outside. The hut was close and smelt of sickness and there seemed to Opio nothing else that he wished to do. He looked once more at the man on the bed, the once powerful body now gaunt and sunken. Magere's eyes were closed and the room was full of his harsh breathing.

Opio went out. He found an empty hut within Magere's

hedge and lay down on the bare floor beside the cold hearth. It was moonlight and the hut only half thatched, for it was being repaired, and the room was full of cold light. He lay and looked at the soot-blackened rafters, like a cage of ribs against the sky, and thought of his uncle. It seemed to him that if Magere died his heart would break.

Presently the women became silent and yet Opio still lay awake. He found himself listening to all the noises of the night, selecting each one from its fellows and listening until he was satisfied that he knew from where it came and what made it: the cicada beetles shrill beneath the bark, the crickets in the furrows and the distant frogs booming at the river's edge. Usually he would no more have heard them than the miller hears the stream that drives his grindstones. Now they seemed to press into the hut and sleep slipped from his grasp like smoke through a child's fingers.

He did not know how long he lay there, but at the end of it sleep was still impossible and he got up and crossed the compound to the house where Magere lay. He meant to go in, but when he reached the doorway he was suddenly afraid of what might be seen there, so he turned aside and waited outside the wall like a child fearing punishment. But still he wanted to know and he sat with his ear against the mud and listened. All was still within, so still that he could hear the white ants eating the beams beneath the daub.

Then he found a hole where the wall had cracked and the dry mud fallen in. In better days it would have been repaired, but now, Opio thought, it did not matter. When Magere was dead the house would be pulled down and nobody might build there again until the death was forgotten.

Opio picked at the mud with a fingernail and then put his eye to the crack and looked in.

There was a little light coming from the fire burning in the middle and more from the moonlight through the open doorway, left unblocked for the man's spirit to escape when it left him. The light from the fire came and went as the flames leapt and fell, but Opio could see well enough. Tapkesos drowsed beside the fire and it crossed Opio's mind that she would have a hard life from the women when Magere died and that he must take her into his own household if her life was to be bearable.

Then he looked at the man on the bed. The eyes were open and glittered and the great chest filled and collapsed as if it would break. Opio's eyes filled with tears and he turned away. Then it seemed to him that he heard his uncle speaking and he wiped his eyes with his fist and looked again. Tapkesos had heard something also, for she had roused and was peering toward the bed. Then she got stiffly to her feet and staggered a little as she walked toward it.

The words seemed to come from far away, but they were clear enough to Opio at the spyhole and they must have been more so to Tapkesos.

"If I'm made to bleed a little I'll live."

She stared down at her husband with no sign of understanding, and the man gasped and struggled for breath and managed again.

". . . bleed a little . . . I'll live."

Then she cried, "But the old man bled you and it did no good."

There was a harsh chuckle from the bed. It died in a fit of weak coughing, then that too passed and there was long silence. Then the voice again, for the moment almost strong.

"Doctors! . . . call them wise but . . . cannot guess my secret. Eh, woman . . . the warriors of your tribe could have told . . . my body doesn't bleed . . . cannot . . . But fast now . . . time . . . little time left. If you love me take my knife . . . there . . . and draw . . . draw a little blood from the shadow on the wall."

She stared at him stupidly and he fought with death before her eyes and pleaded, the voice growing weaker.

". . . if you love me . . ."

Tapkesos turned to the wall. The light from the fire threw Magere's shadow there, distorted by the curve and never quite still because of the flames. She stared at it, then back to the man on the bed, and ran her tongue across dry lips. Opio stared too and lived her fears also. This was magic and might kill.

The strangled voice from the bed pleaded once more. "Do it . . . do it, Tapkesos . . . do it or I'll die . . ."

Then she straightened up and to Opio she looked like the woman who had stood before Magere on the day she had first come to Kano. The fear was gone now and she was beautiful and a Nandi and no fear could touch her. She took the knife from the foot of the bed and went to the wall and Opio watched her try to see the shadow clearly. She must be careful where she used the knife or the man would die as an ordinary soul might die if it were used indiscriminately on his body. Opio understood and willed her skill with all his being and blessed her wisdom. Then, as she hesitated, an undermined log rolled over and flared, and on the bed Magere arched his body and flung an arm up in despair, and quick as a cat she touched the shadow with the sharp point. Both of them heard the great sigh from the bed and saw the spreading stain upon the wall.

Tapkesos dropped the knife and stood trembling. At last she turned and faced the bed.

For a long minute nothing, and Opio, crouching at the wall, grew cramped.

Then Magere smiled at her and his eyes were clean of pain.

"Now," he whispered gently, "you know my secret and hold my life in your hands."

Outside Opio crept away, awed and heavy with a knowledge that he wished had never come to him. Crept back to his bed upon the floor of the unfinished hut, to lie awake.

7

From that moment Magere mended. Within a month he was hale and strong and lively as ever he had been. The place rang with his laughter and when his friends came visiting they staggered when he clapped them on the shoulder and were deafened when he roared for food and beer.

It was night when Tapkesos left him.

She went secretly, while he slept, when the plain was all unguarded and still beneath a moon that was a sister to the one that had watched Opio through the rafters of a hut.

She took nothing except her bracelets and a little of the clothing that had come with her and she slipped away with the light, strong walk of a hill woman, following first the narrow undug strips that separated the fields and then the wild hogs' paths into the hills.

The story of that night's walk, and what followed, is well known because she lived to be an old woman, highly regarded by her people, and she told the tale many times.

She walked with her head held high, knowing herself to be as beautiful as the night. Best of all, her work was complete, or would be in a little while, and she was free. She smiled at her thoughts as she went. Once a leopard coughed near her on the hillside and her heart beat faster, but she was not afraid. It was impossible that anything evil could happen to her now.

Her belief was sound. In the early morning she came safely to some huts of her people, and the young warriors guarding the cattle first challenged and then, when she was recognized, stood silent and adoring, while one of them woke the village.

They gave her milk, clean sour-tasting milk with the bitter tang of charcoal which she had not tasted for a year.

Then they took her to a hut and the young men piled their soft fur cloaks for her to lie on. She was very tired and slept as easily as a child. And while she did so they ran with the news of her return to the cunning ones who ruled the Nandi.

They were not men who came lightly, who could be commanded by a mere warrior, certainly not by a woman. But they came for Tapkesos. They reached the village one by one throughout the morning and when they asked for her, and were told she still slept, they nodded and said she should not be wakened. They sat on the tiny polished stools that were always carried with them and talked sparingly to their equals. The villagers fawned and brought them beer and milk. They sipped and waited patiently.

It was noon before Tapkesos woke. For a moment she stared at the strange roof above. Then she remembered and sat up briskly, and the old woman who had been waiting beside her the morning long smiled with approval. Then she was taken to the old men drowsing in the shade of the eaves outside.

There her story was told and when she cried, "The strength of Magere lies in his shadow!" they nodded and chuckled and blinked eyes which were as wrinkled and old as a lizard's.

Then one old man croaked, "Why didn't you let him die?" and she replied:

"Why should I waste my life? He must be seen to die, and at the hand of a Nandi."

At this they nodded in unison, murmuring: "Good. Good."

After that they dismissed her. "Well done, Tapkesos," said the leader quietly. "Now begin life again where it left off. And get the taste of Luo out of your mouth if you can. You've served us well."

And she smiled at them and went back to her own people, who received her with honor.

The Nandi broke the peace the very night that followed. Kipsaina, the same Kipsaina who hunted with Opio and Magere in the reeds at Kap Narok, was chosen to bring the spear to Kano. He came leaping through the gardens to Magere's village at dawn, at the time that the people were coming sleepily from their houses to work.

He was naked and when he saw them he shouted, "News, dogs, here's news for you."

He flexed his lean hard body, shining black, and hurled the light spear he carried so that it flew in a great curve and stuck quivering in a doorpost. Then he turned and ran like a buck, twisting and swerving from the men who clutched at him angrily.

The oil that covered his body made him impossible to hold.

8

So once again there was war and the Joluo gathered in the way that Magere had taught them. But this time there was no leader with plans and jokes about the coming battle, for Magere stayed in his house and when they came to him for advice he lay on his bed and pulled the corner of a skin across his face and would not answer.

They made a man called Ogot their war leader. He was not a great warrior, being somewhat old for the business, but he was the only man that both clans would accept. There had been tedious wrangling and great bitterness over the choosing, for many men considered themselves fitted to lead. So when they saw that they were not going to get what they wanted they chose Ogot, a man with little ambition and less talent, and after doing so they paid no attention to what he said.

When the Nandi army came down to Kano the Joluo went out beyond the houses and chose a fighting ground close to the foot of the hills, just where the rocks thinned. There they were far from the fields, which were full of young crops that they did not want trampled. But the place was a bad choice, for the Nandi charge when it came would have the weight and speed that comes from sloping ground.

This time the Nandi sang no war-songs. Indeed, they came down in loose formation chattering like hornbills, more like men going to a wedding than to battle. And when they were there, and the two peoples faced each other, they all began calling scornfully for Magere.

"Where is he?" they shouted. "We don't see him. Where's the Stone? Has he grown too fat and short of wind? Does he lie late in bed? Or is he away selling pots at the market? Send for him, dogs. We'll wait."

This last was a mortal insult, because only women made and sold pots.

But when this abuse had gone on for some time and the Nandi still showed no sign of wishing to fight and Opio, listening from his place in the battle line, was ready to die with rage and shame, they suddenly became silent. For a while the Joluo believed that the testing moment had come at last, but then they saw that the Nandi were gazing across the plain, and when they turned their heads to see what interested them they saw that it was Magere.

He had left his hut and, taking spear and shield, had come out to fight. He walked silently through the lines of his own people and on toward the enemy and he looked so sick and broken that even they pitied him and made no attempt to jeer.

When he was before them he lifted his head and asked in a clear quiet voice if there was any man there of the family of Tapkesos who would fight him, and at this, Kilei, the war leader himself, came forward.

"I'm of the same clan as Tapkesos," he said. "I'll fight the Stone."

But this the Nandi would by no means allow and they shouted him down, saying that he was following a private quarrel and that leaders could not be allowed to indulge themselves in this way. So another man was chosen, a brother of Tapkesos called Arap Terer. He was young and tall and eager, and came forward grinning and anxious to make a name for himself.

They met on a smooth stretch of cropped grass in the shade of a half-grown fig tree and both sides leaned on their spears and watched and forgot to breathe. For a minute they circled, sheltering behind their shields, eyes peering across the rims searching for an opening. Then Magere grew weary of this and struck with his spear. He was very slow and Opio was suddenly reminded of the leopard's charge at Kap Narok—there was in both movements the same sense of ruined power and grace. Terer caught and turned the blow easily with his shield. Magere's body was now for a moment unguarded, but the Nandi took no notice of this. Instead he looked down at the shadow before him on the ground. Then suddenly he yelled and drove his spear *there* and danced back. He flung spear and shield away and stood panting and glaring to see what would come of it.

For a moment Magere was still. Then he bent slowly to his knees, rolled on one side. His weapon clattered on the ground and then he was still.

All about the Nandi bayed like a great pack of dogs, seized shields and spears and swept forward in triumph. But Magere's people did not wait for them. They had seen the impossible and they knew that their day was past. Some were caught in the first wave of stabbing triumphant hatred, the rest ran doubling among the trees and rocks.

The Nandi followed swiftly when their first killing was done.

Opio was wounded in the thigh during the first great rush and lay for an hour unnoticed on the field. Later he limped back across the plain to the fields, but there the enemy were about, busy among the houses, so he hid in some half-grown millet and the black smoke of burning thatch drifted over him and stank in his nostrils. He buried his head in his arms and did not greatly care if he was found and killed or not, and the day passed somehow.

But with the coming of night and coolness he felt stronger, and caution returned, and the wish to live. To live at least until he had found Magere and was assured that he was dead. He crept to the edge of the millet to see how the land lay. There were still men moving and he could see the glare of burning houses and so he waited and nibbled the green fingers of grain. Then when it seemed to him quieter he crept out from cover, moving stiffly because of the wound. He felt no hunger, but the long day in the sun had tortured him with thirst and he first made for the river to deal with it. But on the way, beside a ruined hut, he found a broken crock half filled with water and this he drank greedily before turning back again, making for the battlefield.

It was bright moonlight when he reached it.

The dead were still there, for the Joluo had not yet gained enough courage to return and bury them, and the Nandi cared nothing for the dead, either Joluo or their own.

He wandered thoughtfully, looking at still faces, recognizing some.

Presently in front of him a hyena lumbered to its legs and sloped reluctantly away. On reaching the crest of a small rise it turned to snarl.

"Forgive me, hyena," said Opio. "I know this is your night and your world, but I'm looking for a friend."

And he gave a little sob of laughter at his own foolishness in speaking aloud. "Looking for a half of myself," he added.

Then it seemed to Opio that the hyena nodded gravely before trotting off, but it may have been the moonlight, which plays tricks with a man's eyes.

Presently he found the patch of cropped grass and the fig tree.

There was nothing to be seen but a smooth black rock which he did not remember being there before. And Opio believed what he believed and so do all the Joluo.

So Magere left his people what?

A memory of pride, and defeat. A legend, a number of songs and a stone. And one saying. That it is best if a man doesn't trust all his secrets to his wife, no matter how beautiful she is.

"But that is unworthy of him and us," said Opio. "I'd no secrets from Teri while she lived, and was never the worse for it."

Epilogue

A reader is entitled to know whether his book is history, fiction, or, that twilit place between the two, legend.

In this story Victoria Nyanza is, of course, real. So also are the Plain or Valley of Kano and other named places, though some of the minor ones have been transplanted. Kap Narok, for instance, where Opio and Magere hunted a leopard, will not be found in Kano, but on another, greater, valley floor, a hundred miles or so to the east.

All but one of the peoples who appear, the Joluo, Nandi, Samia, Kipsigis, Masai and the rest, exist and live in the places allotted to them. Or, rather, they did, for nowadays tribal boundaries are breaking down and men spill across them and live together, usually at peace. The Snake People *are* somewhat of an invention, but even they bear a resemblance to the people of the Sese Islands, whose warriors have, from time to time, claimed the right to rule the mainland Baganda.

Few people, and perhaps no European, can say with

complete confidence just how these people lived and thought before they were caught up in the wheels of the West, but anyone is permitted a more or less informed guess. After all, the West came to East Africa such a little time ago and one can still meet and speak with old men like Opio who have lived in two worlds. Certainly the rivalry between Joluo and Nandi, here described, existed, and still does; though nowadays it more often finds expression in speeches made by politicians than by spears stabbing among the thorn trees.

But the story.

I first came across the tale of Magere the Stone in an essay written for me by a young Jaluo. When we discussed it I pointed out the resemblance there was to a story from the Old Testament and asked him whether it had been suggested by this. He denied it heatedly. This story was, he declared, that of an episode in Joluo history. He could show me Magere's stone on Kano Plain, even take me to an old man who, as a child, had seen the hero himself in all the pride of his strength. His indignation was real, the similarity I had found obviously novel; I was convinced. And he was right. I never met the old man who had known Magere, possibly he did not exist, but I was to hear the tale told again many times by people who were unlikely to have encountered it other than where all true African stories begin: on the lips of old men and women, beside the dying fire, as night closes in. And I did see the stone. It sits on Kano Plain, where I have put it in this book, and the local people claim that it grinds a finer edge to a spear or knife than the usual run of rocks met there.

Now Africa teems with good stories, the full-flavored brews of men's untutored imagination. They are somewhat out of fashion at the moment, because they are part of the live dark primitive world that is trying to die, and the modern tribesman demands a textbook rather than a story. But they are still there, crowded with wizards and giants and animals that no zoo ever caged; with heroes and gods who came from the snows of the mountains and divided themselves to make men; with snakes that shake the earth when they stir in sleep in the caverns beneath. These tales are strong and old and often cruel and they have the real legendary feel to them. But the Joluo story of Magere is unusual because it is human enough to touch belief. When one has heard it, despite the witchcraft and magic lurking in corners, there remains a conviction that this is about real and recent people and events. Something like it could have happened on Kano in the last century, and I like to believe that it did.

About the Author

HUMPHREY HARMAN first went to Africa in the Second World War and spent most of his time with African soldiers in Africa, Madagascar, and the Far East. Africa seemed to him to be a good place to live and Africans good people to live with and so, when the war ended, he became a schoolmaster, joined the Colonial Education Service, and went to Kenya.

Kenya has been his home for more than ten years. He has served as a District Education Officer and has trained African teachers a few miles from the lake that forms the background of this story.

Mr. Harman writes, "The similarity between the Magere story and the Samson one is remarkable, and I don't pretend to understand it, but this tale didn't come from the Bible. It came from Africa. I didn't put it there, I found it.

"*African Samson* is built around an oral Luo version which is perhaps more circumstantial than most because,

I suspect, a piece of authentic history has been grafted onto the myth. But this last spreads from the Congo to Kenya, and I should hate it to be thought that I claim to have Africanized something which already belongs to the people there."

HUMPHREY HARMAN first went to Africa in the Second World War and spent most of his time with African soldiers in Africa, Madagascar, and the Far East. Africa seemed to him to be a good place to live and Africans good people to live with and so, when the war ended, he became a schoolmaster, joined the Colonial Education Service, and went to Kenya.

Kenya has been his home for more than ten years. He has served as a District Education Officer and has trained African teachers a few miles from the lake that forms the background of this story.

Mr. Harman writes, "The similarity between the Magere story and the Samson one is remarkable, and I don't pretend to understand it, but this tale didn't come from the Bible. It came from Africa. I didn't put it there, I found it.

"*African Samson* is built around an oral Luo version which is perhaps more circumstantial than most because, I suspect, a piece of authentic history has been grafted onto the myth. But this last spreads from the Congo to Kenya, and I should hate it to be thought that I claim to have Africanized something which already belongs to the people there."